VICKY BALL

Content compiled for publication by Richard Mayers of *Burton Mayers Books.*
Cover design by Martiella Design

First published by Burton Mayers Books 2021.


A CIP catalogue record for this book is available from the British Library

ISBN: 978-1-8383459-5-2
Typeset in **Garamond**

www.BurtonMayersBooks.com

# DEDICATION

To David, Hannah and Megan. Your support has meant everything to me.

# ACKNOWLEDGMENTS

To Shenaz, my alpha reader, who read it and encouraged me to go for publication. Your kind words mean so much.

To Richard at Burton Mayers, for believing in me.

A massive thank you to my beta readers - Louise Tollick, Emma Bell, Maddie Bell, Isabelle Dixey, Amelia Francis, Grace Bryson, Chris Malone, Diane Cattermole, and especially to Kerrick Newstead who read it twice. Your detailed feedback had made this novel what it is today.

To my writing group, Mid Week Writers - Dee, Di, Alec, Gemma, Clare, Jan, and Berenice. Your encouragement and feedback have kept me writing for many years.

To my Twitter followers, the Writing Community, thank you for being a huge support and always full of inspiration.

To my parents, Martyn and Gillian, who are 100% behind everything I do.

And finally to my husband David and my daughter's Hannah and Megan. You were my first readers and have supported me and listened to me go on about this for years. Megan, you have been amazing. Your help in creating a website, being my Instagram manager, and giving me editing advice has been invaluable. I could not have done it without you all.

## Part One

# Abby – December 2017

People think I'm an only child. I like being an only child, except I'm not. I may as well be. I haven't seen my sister Beth in seven years. I was eight years old when she disappeared. I don't exactly know what happened, no one will tell me. Was she kidnapped? Did she run away? I have absolutely no idea. She was my age now, fifteen, when she vanished out of my life. I can't say we were that close when she was here. It's hard when there's a big gap. I do remember glimpses of her. Sometimes she was nice to me, like that time when she gave me her lollipop because I dropped mine in the mud; other times she was indifferent. I remember many times trying to show her my latest dance routine, calling and shouting her name to get attention, but she just ignored me. I still remember the frustration I felt. Of course now I understand. If I had an annoying sister who wanted to show me her stupid dance moves I'd probably ignore her too.

I never know what to say when people ask me if I have any brothers or sisters. If I tell them I have a sister then they want to know what she's doing and all that. Most of the time I can't be bothered to explain it again and again. So I tell them I'm an only child. I never say it in front of Mum and Dad. I'm not sure how they'd react, not that they're around much anyway.

They both have full time jobs. Mum used to be a stay at home mum before Beth disappeared but I can barely remember that and it's hard to imagine it now. Dad runs his own business, something boring to do with finance. I switch off when he's on his second sentence of explaining it. Mum is a PA for some grumpy man. I'm not entirely sure what a PA does but I do know she is always answering her phone to him and doing whatever he wants. She may as well be a slave.

What I do know about the day my sister disappeared I found out from my cousin Jo. She told me that Beth bunked off school that day and never came back. Jo never knew if her disappearance was a choice or not. Sometimes I wonder what it would have been like if she had still been here, if Mum hadn't had that fearful look in her eyes all the time.

**Christmas Eve**

It's quite peaceful with chilled out Christmas music on, humming to myself as I carefully place the tinsel on the tree. Carefully place - ha no, that's Dad. I do the tree most years as they are always working till the last minute. I usually just throw it on. I like it kind of haphazard. Dad always complains and ends up rearranging it, says he doesn't want our guests thinking a five-year-old decorated it. How charming is that?

Someone knocks at the door. I almost don't hear it above the music, my humming and the rustling of tinsel. A very thin young woman with pink hair, carrying a big holdall, stands on our doorstep. I don't recognize her for a minute but there's something familiar about her. We both stare at each other until she says, 'Abby?'

Instantly I can see Mum's eyes staring back at me. 'Beth,' I manage to stutter out. This pink-haired wonder is not at all how I'd imagined her

'Yes it's me. Your big sister.'

I'm completely lost for words and stand there dumb, not knowing what to do next.

'Aren't you going to let me in then?'

I stand aside and watch her flounce in as though she's been on holiday or something. I may as well be letting in a stranger. I want to text Olivia with *WHOA you'll never guess who just turned up?* But I doubt she'd even know who she is. I don't talk about her much.

'Where's Mum and Dad?'

'They're at work.' Inside my head, I am screaming. I literally can't believe my long lost sister is standing here in my house, our house. Yet she feels different.

'Both of them?' She dumps her bag, randomly, right where we walk.

I am the queen of messiness, yet it bugs me. 'Yes.'

'Ah, you're decorating the tree. Let me help.' She grabs a bauble and hangs it on the tree. I wouldn't have put it there. I am rooted to the spot in the middle of the lounge.

'Do Mum and Dad know you're coming?'

'Nope. Thought I'd surprise them.'

'Well it'll certainly be that.'

I have so many questions I want to ask yet I can't seem to string a sentence together.

'What time are they getting home?'

'I think they finish early today. Three or four maybe.' I glance at my watch. It's nearly three now.

'Great,' she answers. Full of energy she bounces round the house exclaiming that certain items weren't there before or that some were just the same as she remembers them. I watch her like she is a mirage. She barely pays me any attention, no 'haven't you grown?' or 'you were only a little girl the last time I saw you.' I'm not sure what I want, for her to notice me or for her to leave? Her energy is too much, she can't keep still.

I hear the first key in the door just after three thirty. Beth and I look at each other. Her eyes are lit up with excitement; I feel as though I'm about to witness an explosion.

'Hi Abby, I'm-' Mum stops mid-sentence when she sees Beth. 'Oh I didn't realise you had a friend round.'

Beth stands with a big grin on her face. 'Mum, it's me.'

Mum drops the bags she's been holding. Her mouth whispers, 'Beth?'

Beth nods enthusiastically.

She rushes forward and grabs Beth's arms and head and face, presumably to check she isn't a hologram. Her face is the palest white I've ever seen it. She flings her arms around her. When she finally pulls away, her watery eyes are barely holding it in.

'Oh my goodness I can't believe it. I thought you were- ' She doesn't ask why or where she's been but stands back and touches her hair. 'It's pink- ' She seems to want to say more but she lets go of her. Tears begin to stream down her face and she starts shaking. Frantically she brushes the tears away and smiles anxiously. Through shuddered sobs, she manages to speak. 'You are staying aren't you?'

'As long as you want me.'

'I have to call your father he'll be- '

Mum seems to have lost the ability to speak. I watch as she searches through her handbag for her phone, never for a minute taking her eyes off Beth. 'Oh where is it?' She stops. 'Never mind he'll be home any minute.'

As Beth turns towards the kitchen, Mum mouths excitedly to me, 'she's back.' Her eyes have a sparkle that I've never seen before.

They walk off, arm in arm, towards the kitchen. 'Let me make you a hot chocolate.' I grab the nearest bauble on the tree and throw it angrily on the floor. Mum never makes me a hot chocolate.

A few minutes later, Dad marches through the door. He gives me a quick peck on the cheek and glances over at the tree.

'Thought you'd have finished that by now.'

'I … er … got distracted.' Distracted is an understatement.

'Let me guess: Facebook, no wait sorry, Instagram.'

He ignores my hurt expression and marches off towards the kitchen before I have a chance to reply; in true Dad style, he never could stay in one place for too long. I want to save him for myself before I lose him to the long-lost sister.

He calls back to me: 'Do we have guests?'

'Just one.'

Mum and Beth pop their heads out of the kitchen.

'Look who's here.' Mum's triumphant voice sounds unusually high.

It takes Dad a minute to realise who it is.

'Beth?' He's frozen to the spot. I think I notice a tear in his eye. Then he runs forward and hugs her tight. It's clear he never wants to let her go. 'I can't believe it's you.' They are so happy. But no one asks the big question.

They totter around each other for the next few hours, I twizzle my hair round and round while I watch awkwardly from the corner of the sofa. The way they are talking you'd think she'd just been away on holiday or at university.

'So where have you been for the last ten years?'

They all stop and stare at me. Mum's eyes are wide and accusing.

'Ah you know, here and there,' she answers casually.

'It's alright,' adds Mum quickly. 'You can tell us about it another time.'

'Where's here and there?' I ask, ignoring Mum.

'That's enough,' says Dad firmly.

'Fine, you carry on with your happy reunion then.' And I stomp upstairs.

**Christmas Day**

The first thing I usually do on Christmas morning is run downstairs and open the presents Dad has put under the tree *for me*. I'll have a few special ones in the morning, then the rest later.

This morning is the same except there are no presents under the tree and the tree is still half decorated. In all the excitement yesterday I forgot to finish decorating it or lost motivation to anyway. I search around the tree to find the lost presents but with no luck.

Disappointed, I sit back on my legs. Everyone else is still in bed. According to the clock it is nearly seven, although that clock is hardly reliable. Do I wake Mum and Dad and nicely demand my presents or do I sit here sulking by myself until they wake up, which could be hours?

Dad is snoring when I enter their room. Beth's door is shut which is a strange occurrence. It hasn't been shut for years. I quietly approach their bed and lay my head on Dad's chest, hoping he's had a shower recently and that his grease doesn't rub off on my hair.

'Good morning,' I whisper. He murmurs something incomprehensible and rolls over to face away from me. Oh sod this. I shove him to one side. He still doesn't move so I shove him harder. He starts to come to but I am met with a grumpy expression.

'What is it Abby?'

'It's Christmas Day.'

'Is it?'

I don't know how to say this in a polite way so I come out and say it. 'There are usually presents under the tree.'

Dad sits up suddenly. 'Oh gosh sorry. I completely forgot.' I give him a hurt puppy look. 'So sorry sweetheart. Go back to bed for a few minutes and then Santa might have magically appeared.'

I smile as I sneak back across the hall to my room. Mum is quick to jump to his defence.

'- It's been a busy night. It's not your fault. We hardly slept.'

'I realise that, Emily, but I've never forgotten her presents before.'

That's not quite true. He did forget them once before when I was younger and easily fooled. Back then I used to go into Beth's room and drag her out of bed too. The determination to get what I want is still there.

'What are we going to do about Beth's presents?' I hear him ask.

'What can we do? She can't just turn up and expect presents.' For once I agree with Mum.

'I could pop to the shops.'

'On Christmas Day? There won't be any open.'

'No you're right, silly idea.'

I want to tell him to chill out, that it's only presents and that Christmas isn't just about that, but that's probably hypocritical considering I've woken him up to demand mine.

He shuffles around while I lay in bed patiently. Then I hear a jingling of bells outside my room making me giggle. I leap out of bed and run down the stairs, two at a time. Mum and Dad follow. There are three carefully wrapped presents under the tree. At least they were wrapped and he didn't forget to do that as well. Mum and Dad sit down on the sofa to watch me as I pull them out.

'Should we wake Beth?' asks Dad. I glare at him. I don't want her here.

'She might be tired.' In the end the decision is made for us as we hear footsteps coming down the stairs.

'Oh hi.' She is surprised to see us all. 'Is it present time?'

Dad looks guilty. 'Sorry, we didn't get you anything.'

'Oh of course. That's fine.' But her face tells a different story. What did she expect, that we buy her presents for seven years just in case? She sits down on the sofa next to Mum. Mum puts her arm around her. I shouldn't feel guilty but when everyone is sitting there watching me open my presents I do. I feel bad that I have presents and she doesn't.

'Maybe you could give one of yours to Beth,' Dad whispers to me. I stare coldly at him. You want me to share my presents with the sister who *probably* was dead? But of course I don't say any of that. I reluctantly give her the smallest present. Thank goodness I didn't give her the necklace. Beth's present is a book.

'Oh sorry,' says Dad, turning to me. 'You wanted that

book, didn't you?'

'It doesn't matter,' I say. Of course it does.

'Don't worry you can borrow it after me.' I smile tightly. 'So what are we doing for Christmas?'

'Uncle Pete and Auntie Judy are coming over with Jo and Stephen.'

'Cool. What about Granny and Grandad?'

'They're dead,' I answer coldly.

Dad gives me a death stare. 'Abby!'

'Well they are.'

'Yes but there are better ways to tell her.'

Beth's eyes start to fill with tears. 'It's okay. They were pretty old I guess.'

I want to scream. You don't have a right to care. You walked out on us.

'We better get ready,' says Mum getting up. She pulls Beth tightly to her. 'Do you have something to wear?'

'Yes of course.' I watch as the alien in my family slumps upstairs to get ready.

I spot her upstairs through the gap in the door; watching as she takes clothes out of her bag roughly and chucks them unceremoniously on her bed. They are a weird collection of clothes, all different styles and colours. She sits on her bed and sighs. I consider lending her some of mine; they might fit her except she's skinnier than me. In fact she's super skinny. Did she eat anything in the last seven years? As though she has spotted me, she suddenly pushes the door so it slams, right in my face. Charming!

~

It never occurred to me that my grandparents wouldn't live forever. When Granny died, everyone was shocked and then Grandad went four months later. They had been together for nearly sixty years. I still miss them, Christmas is not the same now. Mum's mum is still alive but she's … well … a bit weird. She sometimes joins us for Christmas but is quite often on a Buddhist retreat or something.

The table is set, Dad standard, when Auntie Judy and

Uncle Pete family arrive. They bundle through the door like a train set on demolishing everything in sight. I love them all, I do, but Pete is loud and Judy asks lots of questions. I like Jo. She is five years older than me and is at university. She tells me everything. Stephen, about three years older than me, mostly doesn't say much.

'So how's my little Abby?' Pete pulls me into a hug, messing up my newly straightened hair. I only spent ages doing it.

'Not so little anymore,' I say, wishing he'd stop hugging me. I wriggle free, smoothing down my hair in attempt to rescue it.

Beth is upstairs, still in the shower.

'So there's something I need to tell you,' Mum announces when the commotion has died down and everyone has taken off their coats and shoes.

'Ooh sounds intriguing.' Pete loves winding his little sister up.

'Um, yes is a bit.' Mum sounds nervous. 'Well it's just that- '

'Beth's home,' I blurt out. Annoyance is written all over Mum's face.

'What?' exclaim both the adults at once. Stephen looks shocked and Jo is mouthing, 'No way,' at me.

'I know, it's huge right?' I'm suddenly enjoying the attention. Probably best to before she gets down here.

'Crazy,' mutters Pete who for once is actually speechless. I laugh a little.

Jo takes me to one side, 'So she's really back?'

'Yes. She turned up yesterday.'

'What? Out of the blue?'

'No warning, nothing, on our doorstep.'

'I'm surprised your Mum and Dad didn't faint.'

'I think they almost did.'

Mum and the adults have moved into the kitchen. Pete, having found his tongue, is firing repeated questions at her.

'Did she say where she's been?' asks Jo. Her eyes are still wide.

'Nope. Got nothing out of her.'

'I can't believe this.'

'Me neither.'

Beth appears, glamorous and made up, pink lipstick to match the pink hair.

'Hi everyone.'

Pete appears and stops before her, staring at her.

'Blimey, look at you, all grown up. What a stunner.'

Auntie Judy hugs her without a word while Jo and Stephen stare at her awkwardly.

'Well, you clearly had enough money,' remarks Pete, his eyes darting up and down her. I wonder how he can tell that just from looking at her. 'Still got that older fellow of yours?' Mum shoots him a death stare.

'Why don't we get some drinks?' suggests Mum guiding them towards the kitchen. 'I'll show you what we've got.'

With the adults gone, Beth stands there smiling at Jo who has not said a word to her. From what I remember and from what Jo told me, her and Beth used to get on really well.

'So how you doing?' Beth asks Jo.

'Fine. I'm at university.'

'Cool. What are you studying?'

'Architecture.'

'That sounds amazing.'

'What about you Beth? Have you been working?'

'Yeah this and that.' What does this and that even mean?

'Love the hair.' Jo's eyes full of admiration. Beth flicks it back dramatically.

We don't get any more out of her as Mum rings the bell for dinner. We shuffle to the table. I am about to sit in my usual seat when Beth gets there first. I stand there awkwardly. She turns to face me.

'Oh sorry, is this your seat?'

'No it's fine.'

I move to the other side. The great thing about my seat is that you have a perfect view of the garden. It could have been her seat before she left, I don't remember.

'A toast to us,' says Dad when we are sat down.

'And to my long-lost sister,' I add sarcastically. Everyone raises their glasses, glancing around awkwardly. Beth smiles.

Later she corners me in the corridor as I'm about to go to the toilet.

'I'm sorry if I'm usurping you.'

'Usur- what?'

'Usurping: it means pushing someone out of their throne position. You are acting a bit put out that I'm here.'

'Well I- ,' I begin.

'The thing is I was here first.' I want to point out that I have lived here for the last seven years so technically I have already usurped her.

'You can't just turn up here and expect it all to be the same,' I say bravely, trying to ignore her increasingly angry expression.

'I never expected that.'

I shrug my shoulders and raise my eyebrows at her as if it's a challenge.

'You have no idea what it was like.'

'Then tell me. I'm not a kid anymore.'

She sighs. 'Everyone hated me.'

'Everyone?'

'Mum, Dad, you.'

'Me? I was eight.'

'Okay, maybe not you but everyone else. I had to get out of here.'

'For seven years?'

'It's complicated.'

Uncle Pete interrupts us. 'Hey Beth Kimmings we need you. You are the monopoly champion if I remember rightly.'

'Oh yes I am. Prepare to be in debt.'

Pete drags her away, his arm around her. She shrugs him off, suddenly looking very uncomfortable with his attention.

**Boxing Day**

When I wake up I swear I can hear screaming coming out of Beth's room. Not full on horror movie but faint little screams and protests as if she is having a nightmare or something. I'm still in half sleep mode so maybe I'm dreaming.

On Boxing day we would normally go to Pete and Judy's house, but this year Mum decides it would be too much too soon for Beth. It would be better to have a quiet day at home. Better for who? I was looking forward to seeing Jo again. Instead we are sat watching bad Christmas movies with only Christmas dinner leftovers to eat.

'Are you not eating that?' Beth has spent most of the meal pushing her food around the plate. Mum never seems to care that much when I eat dinner.

'Not hungry.'

Then Beth decides it's too much family fun and goes upstairs to lie down. The bags under her eyes this morning suggests she didn't sleep well.

'Don't you want to know where she's been for the last seven years?' I ask after she's gone.

'Of course,' replies Mum 'but you can't rush these things. She'll tell us in her own time.'

'If it were me I'd just ask her.'

'And risk her running away again?' Dad states robotically.

'So she wasn't kidnapped then?'

'Not technically, no.'

'Not technically? What does that mean?'

Dad sighs. 'Oh Abby, leave it. We'll talk about it another day.'

'That's what you always say and we never do.'

'That's because maybe there aren't always answers,' Mum shouts and storms out to the kitchen, taking it out on the plates. Dad glares at me as if it were my fault.

I don't think it's too much to ask to expect answers.

In the afternoon we are sitting on the sofa watching a cheesy Christmas movie, playing at being a happy family. I'm still feeling grumpy that we aren't at Pete and Judy's house. By now they will be playing an epic game of Risk which I would most likely lose but I don't care.

The film finishes. I snigger at the sight of Dad snoring away in his chair in the corner. Mum smiles at me and shrugs.

'I'm pretty tired,' yawns Beth. 'I'm going to have a nap.' How many naps does this girl need?

'What do you want to watch?' Mum asks me.

'Dunno.'

She flicks through the channels.

'Oh wait, stop. Shrek. Let's watch that,' I yell. I may be a teenager but you gotta love Shrek, obviously don't tell my friends.

We get half way through the film when we hear shrieks coming from up the stairs. Mum jumps up.

'Beth are you okay?' She runs up the stairs. I sit up, puzzled. Dad wakes up. 'Huh?' I run up after Mum. Dad is left confused on his own while Donkey argues with Shrek on the TV.

When I get up there Beth is sobbing her eyes out, Mum is holding her close.

'It's alright now,' she repeats continuously.

'What's going on?' I mouth to Mum.

She waves me away and pushes the door closed. The room is completely dark. I stand outside and listen. Gradually Beth's sobs begin to lessen and decipherable words come out of her mouth.

'He texted me again. He won't leave me alone.'

'Who won't?'

'I just wanted to get away from him.'

'Who dear? Tell me.'

'I can't tell you. You wouldn't understand.'

'I might if you let me try.'

'No Mum, stop it. You can't fix it.' Her voice is beginning to rise. She sounds angry. 'You think you can fix everything. It's not like that. Leave me alone.'

'Please Beth, I only want to help.'

'Get out,' she yells.

'Okay, I'm here if you want to talk.'

'Get out!' she screams again.

Mum emerges, tear stained, shrugging at me helplessly. I pull Mum to me in a hug as she goes by. She pats me on the shoulder and carries on, throwing me a grateful look.

Whatever has happened with Beth is still going on. Who is this man who won't leave her alone? I wonder if she will talk to me but I daren't go in there now for fear of being shouted at.

Mum and Dad are having a heated quiet discussion (AKA argument) when I get downstairs. If it were not for Beth upstairs they would probably be screaming at each other by now. Despite my presence they carry on. Shrek is singing about his swamp.

'We need to talk to her,' Mum is saying urgently. 'We can't leave her like that.'

'She's not ready to talk.'

'Jack, she needs to talk. We need to know what's going on.'

'We have to be patient.'

'I'm sick of being patient. She can't swan back in here and not tell us anything.'

'What, so you just want to give her an ultimatum, tell us what's going on or get out, because that worked out so well last time.' He sighs.

'And why is she so thin? She barely ate anything at lunch. Do you think she's got an eating disorder?'

'Emily leave it. You worry too much. I'm sure she's

fine.'

I am afraid; once more my world has been turned upside down and all those memories of similar conversations from seven years ago are starting to creep back in. Mum and Dad arguing, screaming, crying. It's happening again.

Suddenly aware of my presence, Dad changes his tone. 'Let's talk about this later.'

'I'm not a child anymore, you know,' I say.

'Sorry love but it's- '

'I know, I know, complicated.'

I walk away in a huff. I know I shouldn't, but I feel angry too. I wish someone would tell me what's going on.

**December 27th 2017**

Shuffling outside my door wakes me up. For a moment I forget what has happened in the past few days, forget that my sister has returned, but then it all comes flooding back and I'm not sure how I feel about it.

Whimpering sounds coming from Beth's room make me sit up. I've never noticed how thin the walls are in this house until now. I can practically hear everything in her room. 'Please stop,' she is saying. Should I go in there? Then I hear Mum's soft voice clearly soothing her back to sleep. I'm not used to sharing Mum with anyone.

'It's alright. It's a dream.' She says it as though it is a magic wand. Does she really think that saying that will make everything okay? 'Go back to sleep now.'

It seems to work though as soon after I can hear the gentle purring of Beth sleeping.

While Mum is distracted I take the opportunity to sneak downstairs to retrieve my phone. I know she'll be mad. According to her phones in rooms before nine am are a bad idea. What does she know? Why am I the only one who has to charge my phone downstairs at night? Literally all my friends are allowed to keep theirs. It is so unfair. I climb back into bed, under the warm covers, hidden away.

*So glad to have my long lost sister back home with us (Smiley face).* I post it on Facebook without even thinking but straight away a tiny bit of guilt pops into my head. Should I be doing this? Is Mum or Beth or both going to be mad at me? I consider deleting it but already I notice it is liked by two people. No point in taking something down which people want to see. The comments come flying in:

*Amazing news.*

*Great you must be so happy.*

*I didn't even realise you had a sister.*

*You have a sister?*

*Where's she been all this time?*

*Was she the one that was kidnapped?*

*Didn't you think she was dead?*

Maybe I shouldn't have posted it. I mean she's only just got here. What if she leaves because I told everyone? What if I scare her off? But as the comments pile in, I shrug off the negative thoughts; I can't delete it now. Most people know already. Eventually bored of lying in bed and scrolling pointless posts on Facebook I creep downstairs, feeling hungry, in search of breakfast. Mum is sitting at the breakfast bar gazing intently at her phone. The stern eyes and tight lips as she turns to me says all I need to know. She's read the post.

'Why did you put it on Facebook?'

I shrug. 'Wanted to share the great news,' I say sarcastically. I don't mean to be sarcastic but it comes out that way.

'I have had about three different people already texting me about it. You don't think that maybe I would have wanted to tell them?'

'Sorry I didn't realise.'

'No, you didn't. You don't think, you do things and don't even consider the consequences.'

The attack seems unjustified. All I did was post on

Facebook. Now she's trying to make me out to be some kind of enemy.

'It's no big deal.'

'Clearly not to you. Don't know how Beth's going to react to this.'

'It's always about Beth isn't it?' I say, storming out without getting any breakfast.

I hide out in my bedroom, fighting off tears but determined not to show it to Mum. She appears at my door ten minutes later.

'I'm sorry I shouted at you,' she begins, the tears threatening to fall. 'It's a very stressful time.'

'I'm sorry too,' I answer, though I'm not sure how sorry I am.

'Listen, I have to go to work now. Dad's already gone but if you want me to stay, to look after you guys, I will.'

'We'll be fine. I am fifteen now and well Beth's a teensy bit older than that now. I think we can take care of ourselves.'

'Call me if you need anything.'

'Of course.'

Hearing the door slam a little later, I realise it's not even nine am. I should be in bed, sleeping, like any other normal teenager. I make my way downstairs and position myself on the sofa with my cereal as I load up Netflix. Mum hates me eating in the lounge, fearing that I will make a mess on the sofa/carpet. When I have my own house I won't get stressed about sofas and carpets. There's more to life.

I'm fully engrossed in the latest series I've started watching, while texting Olivia, when the lounge door opens, making me jump. I had forgotten that Beth was even here. She smiles shyly at me. I stare at her for a moment. Our first day alone together. This could be good or bad. I decide to smile back.

'What you watching?' she asks.

'Oh some series about vampires.'

'Cool.'

'Yeah.'

My phone pings. She leans over and spots the message on Instagram.

'Who's that messaging you?'

'Just some guy.' Her face turns white.

'Do you know him?'

'No, should I?' I reply.

'So he's a stranger?' I nod. 'What are you going to do?'

'Nothing. Ignore him.'

'You need to be careful. Maybe you should block him,' she says quickly.

'Why are you making such a big deal about this? I can handle it. It happens all the time.'

She doesn't say anything but when a text comes through she bites her lip and stares at it.

'It's Mum,' I explain. No doubt Mum wants to apologise yet again.

*Sorry about earlier. How are you both doing?*

*Fine,* I reply.

*How's Beth?*

*She's good.*

*What are you up to?*

*Not much*

I know she expects some essay answer but what is there to say? But there is no way I can tell her what we're talking about.

*Be good. Phone me if you need me.*

I don't reply. As I put my phone down the house phone rings. Really? Can a girl not relax for a second? I glance over at Beth. Maybe she should answer it now, she's the older one but she looks terrified. Clearly that's not going to happen. Reluctantly I get up. It's Uncle Pete.

'Hi Abby, how's it going?'

'Fine.'

'How's the runaway sister doing?'

'She's fine,' I say, sneaking a glance at Beth. Well she

was crying in her sleep this morning. But I can't say that of course.

'Ring me if you need anything.'

'I will,' I answer bemused. Does everyone suddenly think I'm incapable of looking after myself since Beth returned? I mean I've been doing it for years. I hang up and return to the sofa.

'Who was that?'

'Oh, only Uncle Pete.'

'Oh right. Is he good?'

'Think so.'

She reaches over and grabs her phone from the corner where she has been charging it all night.

'You thought you'd announce it to the world did you?' She slams her phone on the coffee table, making me jump.

'What?'

'You put it on Facebook.'

'I thought you weren't on Facebook,' I answer quickly, feeling my face getting hot.

'I'm not.'

'Seemed a good idea at the time.'

'You don't think I would have liked to have enjoyed my first few days in peace and quiet?' Her voice is getting louder. 'You don't think I would want to be safe?'

She gets up and runs loudly up the stairs, slamming her bedroom door, leaving me wondering what she meant by safe. Is she in danger? Should I go after her? I could delete the post but it's too late for that. I bury myself in the blanket and carry on watching Netflix. I am beginning to wish I was still an only child. Life was a lot simpler then.

A key in the door interrupts episode seven of season one.

'Hi girls,' Mum calls. 'Oh hi Abby. Where's Beth?'

'Upstairs.'

'Everything okay?'

'Yep,' I say while continuing to stare at the screen.

Giving up, she goes to the kitchen. I hear sobbing.

'What's wrong Mum?' I yell, reluctantly moving towards her.

Embarrassed, she tries to brush away the tears.

'I'm fine, really, don't worry.' She's clearly not so I put my arm around her. She rests her head in my arms. 'I'm such a failure,' she sobs.

'No way. Why are you a failure?'

'Because it's my fault she went away and I can't even help her now.'

'What do you mean it's your fault?' She steps away from me.

'It doesn't matter. Thanks for the hug.' She runs upstairs before I can question her further.

Why do I feel like everyone is keeping secrets?

**New Years Eve**

Home is a weird place right now. Mum and Dad are tiptoeing around us as if Beth is fragile and about to break. Who can blame them? It's been a long time. Like me they must have so many questions. I feel bad, I'm not being very nice to her but this is my house. I have always been the one who calls the shots but the balance has shifted. She looks at me with this worried expression and I wonder if she's in trouble or something. I don't even know where to start in talking to her. She's a stranger to me.

Mum is talking loudly on the phone downstairs. She thinks she's being quiet but I can practically hear every word.

'We were as shocked as anyone … yeah, she just turned up totally out of the blue … no, of course I didn't. I didn't want her to run away again … I know, I know. I'll have to have that conversation, just not yet.'

Good old subtle Mum. Beth pads lightly by my room, peering in the open door and smiling at me. I guess she can probably hear every word too. Mum finds Beth in the hallway.

'So tonight me and Dad are going out for dinner. If you want to come I can call them and see if they'll add on another person.'

'What about Abby?'

'She's going to Olivia's house, her friend from school. She might let you go with her if you ask her.'

Um excuse me? Maybe I don't want my strange sister gate-crashing Olivia's party.

'I think I'll just stay at home and chill out. I'm pretty tired anyway.'

Thank goodness for that! I hear Mum's footsteps retreating down the stairs. Ten minutes later she is shouting back up.

'Almost time for lunch.' I walk downstairs in anticipation of the much promised sandwiches.

'Can you tell Beth it's lunch time?'

I sigh. 'Beth,' I shout up the stairs. 'It's lunchtime.'

'No, I mean actually go up there and tell her.'

'But I just got down here.'

I drag myself up the stairs grumpily.

As I push open Beth's door she throws something on the floor, a book.

'What you doing?'

'Nothing.' I can just make out the author, Jacqueline Wilson. Nothing to be ashamed of, I did stop reading it about three years ago though. I glance around the room. I've never realised how little has changed in this room. It's still painted in a sickly pink colour with flowery borders. The bed has the same yellow sunshine patterned duvet cover on it. I guess she must have picked it. Would she still pick the same one now? I'm not sure.

'Mum says to tell you that she's made some sandwiches for lunch if you want them.'

'Thanks.'

As I turn to leave, a memory flashes before my eyes, me jumping on Beth's bed demanding to be tickled, Beth laughing, me giggling. For a minute I wish I was that little girl, I miss the old Beth. Any hope I had of grabbing the sandwich and going back up are dashed when I see Mum and Dad sitting at the dining table. Mum pats the chair next to her indicating that Beth should sit there. That feeling of hurt rears its head.

'I made your favourite, cheese and pickle.'

Would Mum even know what my favourite sandwich was?

I start munching through my sandwich, eager to get it over with. I notice Beth staring at me strangely.

'What?'

'Nothing. Just you're a fast eater.'

'Yes, and?' Why do I get the feeling she's mocking me? At least I eat, I want to reply but don't.

'So Beth,' Mum starts, trying to change the subject. 'Do you fancy going for a walk after lunch?'

'In the woods?' she asks.

'Yeah sure. Abby will come too won't you?'

A walk, seriously?

'If I have to.'

'We'll all go,' adds Mum. 'It'll be fun.'

'Actually I've got work to do,' interrupts Dad. 'You go. Don't let me stop you having fun.' Mum looks disappointed but not surprised. He seems to spend a lot of time working.

Although the idea of a walk seems so repulsive I must admit being outside does lift my spirits slightly. Maybe fresh air is good for you.

To look at us you would assume we were a normal happy family. No one could even begin to suspect the stuff that has gone on in the last seven years. The path narrows and I lead the way, allowing Beth to walk behind next to Mum.

'You know Beth we're here if you need to talk about anything,' Mum offers.

'I will but not yet.'

Mum chats away until we reach a clearing.

'You used to love climbing this tree do you remember?' Beth shakes her head but I wonder if she's lying. 'You loved doing that kind of thing.' Mum glances up at the tree, smiling.

'Mum, I'm twenty two now.'

'I understand that,' she answers defensively.

Does she though? Does she wish she had her fifteen year old Beth back instead of this strange creature before us?

'I don't remember this.' Beth touches the wooden play area that we have just reached.

'This was built about six years ago,' says Mum.

I don't remember it not being here. What's going through her head? Is she remembering all the times she came here? Did she ever come here with a boyfriend?

It's getting dark so we turn back. I put my arm through Mum's, possessive I know, but she's my Mum. I don't want to lose that. Mum smiles awkwardly. I want to scream out that I was here first except I wasn't. Beth was.

The warmth of the house sucks us in, a warm blanket ready to comfort us. With red cheeks and icy cold fingertips, we are grateful when Mum immediately puts on the kettle.

'I'm sorry,' Beth's voice is quiet and soft. I am not expecting it.

'For what?'

'For coming here and disrupting your life, for leaving it in the first place.'

'I cried every night when you left.' It's true. I don't like to remember those times. I was so young but my big sister went away.

'You did?'

'I just wanted to cuddle you.' To my horror tears begin to fall down my face. 'I thought you were dead. No one would tell me anything.' I try to push away the tears but it's too late.

'Oh Abby.' She pulls me close to her, her tears

mingling with mine. 'I'm so sorry.'

It's so confusing. The old Beth is gone now. This new Beth, which is like the old one, is back but she doesn't feel the same anymore.

When Mum comes in with the hot drinks we are a sobbing mess on the sofa. Putting them down, she hugs us both. I sit up and wipe my tears.

**New Year's Day 2018**

I wake up on Olivia's mattress on her floor, lying awkwardly. My head hurts, not due to the alcohol, I hardly had any, but due to the late night and the restless sleep full of mixed up dreams. I can't believe Olivia's parents left alcohol in the house. They trusted her, apparently.

I worried about Beth last night, feeling bad for leaving her. When she first came back I wanted to hate her. How dare she leave us and expect to walk right back in. After our little cry together, we have turned a corner or maybe a little bend. Something about the way she looked at me, eyes wide with fear, told me there was more to the story. I've started to remember things as well. Little things about Beth, the way she cuddled me in bed when I had nightmares and how she could make the best cheese on toast ever. I'm dying to get home again.

'You sleep alright?' asks Olivia.

'Hmm okayish. You?'

'Like a log. I was so tired. Great party though.' I nod. It was an alright party. Some friends came, the parents were out, it was hardly the promised wild party. The others slept in the spare room as Olivia's room is tiny.

'I'm gonna make some pancakes for breakfast,' she announces, leaping out of bed.

I must admit Olivia does make pretty good pancakes. We giggle as she flips the pancake in the air barely missing the light fitting above.

'You're lucky that didn't end up on the ceiling,'

comments Erin. We laugh. For a short while I am able to forget about my worries until Olivia asks the question they are probably dying to know.

'So Beth's back. Where did she go?'

Their eyes eager, hopeful that I will divulge something exciting. I wouldn't tell them even if I did know. They are only in it for the sensationalism. Ooh look at me, big words!

I shrug. 'I don't know. She has told me nothing.' Which is almost true.

'Do you think she ran away?' asks Erin.

'Who knows!' I answer non-committedly.

'But don't you want to know?' asks Emma.

'Of course, but she'll tell me in her own time.' I can see they are not done with this conversation so I swiftly change the subject. The latest episode of Love Island is enough to steer them well clear of it. I am glad as I was about to start snapping at them. I don't want to fall out.

By ten I am desperate to go home but we are watching some dumb show on Netflix. I debate whether it would look rude if I suddenly upped and left. It would be good to see Beth before Mum and Dad get back from their overnight party.

I wait half an hour before making my apologies.

'Aw Abby, you can't go yet,' moans Olivia. 'I was going to make a toastie for lunch with my new toastie maker.' She points to the kitchen alluringly.

I am almost tempted by the thought of the melted cheese but I have to go.

'Sorry guys but I have to get back.'

I take my clothes into the bathroom and pull yesterday's clothes on. They are smelly but I don't care. I wave at my friends, still glued to Netflix they barely notice me. The fresh air on the short walk home wakes me up.

Beth is lying on the sofa also watching Netflix when I arrive home. I smile at the mirror image of where I have just left.

'Hi,' I say, plonking myself next to her. She looks up and smiles slightly.

'How was your night?' I ask.

'Boring but hey.'

'Sorry.'

'Not your fault.'

Wondering how to bring it up again, I spit out 'So did you want to talk about anything?' feeling as though I am the stupidest person alive.

'Not really.'

'Yesterday you said you wanted to talk.'

'That was yesterday,' she murmurs, eyes still fixed straight ahead.

'Oh right.' I am disappointed. 'Well, I'm here if you do need to talk.' Ugh, now I'm starting to sound like Mum.

Realising I'm going to get nothing more from her, I go upstairs and climb into bed. I'm so tired that when I lie down I am barely able to keep my eyes open.

Mum wakes me up with a big smile, asking if I want some lunch.

'Oh you're home?' I ask, confused.

'We got back about half an hour ago. You must have been tired.'

'Yeah, didn't get much sleep.'

'I don't know why they call them sleepovers may as well be called wakeovers.'

'Tell me about it.'

'Anyway, lunch?'

'Yeah, sure.'

She disappears downstairs to fulfil my order. I turn over, intent on getting a tiny bit more sleep, when Beth appears at the door.

'Can I come in?'

'Of course.' She sits on the end of my bed awkwardly.

'Sorry if I've been a pain.'

'You haven't,' I say, even though she has.

'Well anyway. It's been so tough these past seven years.

I don't really feel I can talk to anyone.'

'You can talk to me.'

A tear escapes from her right eye. 'I don't want to put you in danger.'

'Why would I be in danger?'

'It's complicated. So hard to explain.' I roll my eyes at that word again; it's always complicated. 'There are people after me.'

'What kind of people?'

'Bad people.'

'Beth, I'm not five.'

'You may not be five but I doubt you could even imagine what they want. I hope you couldn't. I don't know why I'm telling you this. You're still a kid.' She must have caught my annoyed expression as she adds, 'you are. I'm sorry but this was a mistake.' She gets up to leave.

'No wait. I want to help.'

'I know you do,' she adds turning away and leaving.

I lie in bed troubled by Beth's words and in a dilemma. Do I tell Mum or Dad? But surely they must know.

**January 2nd 2018**

'I'm off to work,' Mum calls from the hallway, waking me up from my sleep. Why does she have to do that? I'm not even back at school for a few more days. One less lie-in for me. I bury my head in my pillow and try to get back to sleep but it's not happening.

Grumpily I take myself down the stairs, grab some cereal and switch on the TV to find Jeremy Kyle repeats. Beth is already in the kitchen making coffee so I'm glad I can claim the TV. These days I can never be sure of getting it. It used to be all mine.

'You don't watch this rubbish do you?' she calls from the kitchen.

'It's funny.' The words *My daughter slept with my brother and my dad* flash up on the bottom of the screen and I have to smile. Bit gross but that's why it's funny.

'It's trash,' she says harshly.

'I like it.' She doesn't reply.

'So, what are you doing today?' she asks finally. I look around me as though to say *do I need to do anything today?* 'I might go into town, spend those vouchers from Uncle Pete. Wanna come?' she offers.

'Actually I might. Give me half an hour.'

'I was thinking more like an hour. No rush.'

'Cool.'

Admittedly it would be good to get out. Going around town with my big sister will be a novelty I'm not used to.

It's an hour and a half before we leave for the bus. It feels weird, having not been out properly in days. Beth is wrapped up warm with her big coat and scarf. My thin jacket is not enough but I'd rather look good than be warm. I might meet someone I know.

'Aren't you cold?' she asks.

'No it's good.' She doesn't look convinced.

A bus arrives, one of those double decker types that looks like it could do with a bit of updating. I hope we don't get the driver who hurtles round the corners at one hundred miles an hour. Sitting on the bus with my sister next to me is an odd sensation but not an entirely unwanted feeling. A sense of pride comes over me. This is my sister.

It's a twenty minute journey past the posh houses nearer town, the ones everyone would love to live in but can't afford. Fortunately we seem to have a good driver, friendly too.

'Didn't you go there?' I comment as we pass her old grammar school. The school sits high on the hill to the right of us, an old building, completely different to my modern school.

'Yeah I did.'

'You don't sound too enthusiastic about it,' I joke.

'Hmm. Was a bit stressful to be honest. How come you

didn't go there?'

'I'm not the one with the brains in the family. You were the smart one.'

'Didn't turn out so smart though, did I?' We both smile. I wonder what her life would have been like if she had stayed at school, if she had stayed at home.

'Stressful how?'

'Oh you know, a lot of pressure to get top grades. If you got less than an "A" you were failing.'

I can't even imagine getting one "A" let alone all "A"s. I would hate to be in such a school with nerds. Must be so dull.

We are getting on so well that I consider asking her about the past seven years but I don't. I'm afraid of her response. I'm afraid she'll shut down again.

Town is pretty busy, red sale signs screaming at you from shop windows and some old man shouting something about two bags of chestnuts for a pound. He can keep his chestnuts, it's the clothes I'm interested in.

'Ooh don't you love that top?' I point at a red top in the window of New Look. It would go great with my new jeans I bought last week.

'It's alright.' I'm disappointed at her lack of enthusiasm. Why doesn't she love it like I do? I mean it's gorgeous.

I drag her into the shop anyway. She stands there awkwardly as I rifle through the sale rails, well I mean it would be rude not to check them out. Then suddenly out of the blue she pulls me down to the floor. My arm hits the floor with a thump.

'Hey, what are you doing?'

'Seen someone from school,' she whispers. 'I don't want them to see me.'

'That was years ago. Why do you care what they think now? Are you okay? Your hands are shaking!'

'Shush, I'm fine. Bad memories that's all.'

I try to peer up to see the said person but she pulls me down again. 'No, not yet.' She puts a finger to her lips.

She's starting to scare me now. This is more than just a friend or enemy from school. She gets up slowly and then lets out a breath, she must have been holding it in all this time.

'They've gone. Sorry about that.'

'What's going on?'

'Nothing.' I pull myself to a standing position. Whoever it was has gone now. I never found the red top but I've lost enthusiasm for it now.

We stay in town for an hour more but Beth appears on edge the whole time. I try to distract her with a cappuccino in Costa but it's clear she doesn't want to be there. She barely listens to a word I say.

Finally, I announce we are done. Beth looks like she can't get out of there fast enough.

**January 3rd 2018**

I hate going back to school after the holidays. It feels as though it is the middle of the night when you wake up; it's cold and basically it's just not Christmas anymore. There is nothing to look forward to. I trudge to school, tired and cold. My friend Katie surprises me from behind.

'Hey you.' I turn and smile wearily at her. 'What's up, you look miserable.'

'January blues,' I answer.

'It'll be Easter soon.'

That thought cheers me slightly, lots more chocolate, hmm!

'I see you had an exciting Christmas.'

I stare at her, unsure.

'Your long lost sister returned?!'

'Oh, yeah that.'

'Don't seem too happy. I thought you'd be over the moon. I would be if my long lost sister returned.'

'You don't have a sister.'

'But if I did.'

'Well anyway, it's weird.'

'Why weird?'

'I dunno. She's acting strange. Something's going on and she won't tell me.'

'Did you find out why she went? Was she kidnapped?'

'I still have no idea.'

'Can't you just … you know … ask her?' She says it like she's the only one who has come up with this idea.

'Of course I have but she says I'm too young to understand.'

'I hate it when people say that. We're not babies anymore.'

'I know!'

Before we get to school I am bombarded by no less than ten people, all wanting to know about my long lost sister. I could be a celebrity, next they'll be getting me to sign autographs. Even the teachers have something to say about it.

'Great news about your sister, Abby.' I smile uneasily at my form tutor, who I know means well, but when she comes out with stuff like that she sounds creepy. In fact any teacher talking to you and pretending to care sounds creepy.

I find it hard to concentrate on lessons, constantly wondering what Beth is doing and what is going to happen next. Will she stay home and get a job? I have mixed feelings about her sticking around. She's my sister but it feels like a stranger is living in my house. I wonder if life will ever be normal again.

'Hey Abby, I heard your sister is back.' It's Martha who is totally full of herself. She probably hates that I am getting all this attention.

I try to ignore her but she follows me.

'Where's she been all this time?'

'Back off will you.'

'Ooh, who's got brave now her big sister is back?'

'Yeah, and you know what, she'd have you.' I don't

think she would but it feels good to say it.

'Is that a threat?'

Luckily I am saved by Mr Donovan, the deputy head.

'Get to class you lot. You're going to be late.'

Martha throws me one last look before turning the other way. I find that I am shaking a little. I'm not used to confrontation. Why do some girls have to be so bitchy?

The day goes by achingly slow. Somehow erosion and literary devices don't seem that important anymore. I try to brush off the teachers who keep picking on me for questions. Can't they see that I'm not listening?

Beth is outside the school gate as I leave for home.

'What are you doing here?'

'I thought I'd come and walk with you.' She says it lightly but her expression doesn't match.

I raise an eyebrow. 'I can walk myself you know.'

'Of course you can but you never know who's out there,' she jokes, but something about her tone unnerves me.

'I think most people are more in danger of us school kids than the other way round.' I glare over at Martha and her friends cackling like a gaggle of witches.

Beth smiles. 'You might be right.'

Every now and then, Katie who is walking with us, stares at Beth, she must find it hard to believe she's real. I guess to most of my friends she was always a fictional character from the past. I actually think most of them thought I'd made her up. 'Did you have a good day?' asks Beth.

'Yes Mum,' I mock.

She throws her hands in the air. 'Just asking.'

'No I hardly see *her* lately.'

'When did she go back to work?'

'I don't remember. I feel like she's always worked. Sometime in primary school I guess. Mrs Purvis used to pick me up then.'

'Oh no not Mrs Purvis!'

We both laugh.

'Who's Mrs Purvis?' asks Katie.

'She's this crazy old lady from two doors away who has ten cats and gets her hair permed, like every week.'

'Actually she was pretty good to me. She even updated the biscuits when I came round.'

'You mean you didn't have those soft ones that were six months old?'

'No I didn't.' We are both laughing our head off. Vague twinkles of memory come into my head as I remember the times when we went over there.

'Didn't she have a poodle back then or something?' I ask.

'Yes. We used to walk it. Don't you remember?'

'Just. I was only eight.'

'I forget you were so young. I can remember everything.'

I put my arm through hers forgetting that Katie is still with us. It feels good to have a sister again.

**January 4th 2018**

Another day of school. I'm so tired. I hate getting out of bed. Who's stupid idea was it to make school start at 8.30am? Far too early for a teenager. They must know that we need our sleep. The day drags slowly. Thankfully, most people seem to have forgotten that my long lost sister has returned. I'm already old news. I wish I could say the day was interesting or even useful. The only good part is lunchtime when I get to hang out with my friends.

'So, is your sister staying?' asks Olivia when we are alone.

I shrug. 'No idea.'

'Do you want her to?'

'I guess. I don't know. Not sure what's going to happen.'

'What do you mean?' I tell her about the thing that

happened in the shop. 'Are you sure you're not reading too much into this and imagining more drama than there is.'

'You didn't see her. She looked terrified.'

'Well, I guess you know her.'

'I'm not so sure anymore.'

'Maybe you should ask her about it.'

'I've tried but she always says she's fine but she's clearly not and I don't want to hassle her about it. I don't want to be Mum.'

She laughs. 'Ooh can you imagine. We turn out like our Mums.'

'A fate worse than death.' We both chuckle.

When I get home, Beth's eyes are puffy and her face is red; she's been looking more and more upset since our trip to town. It feels like she is slipping away again. Something is bothering her and I don't know what.

I know I shouldn't but I have got into the habit of eavesdropping on her conversations with Mum. I prefer to call it being a detective. She's in the kitchen at the moment, sitting on that dodgy stool, the one that should have been replaced years ago. It's probably been there since she left, if not before. Starving and desperate to raid the cupboard for a chocolate bar I hold back, deciding instead to listen to their conversation from the hallway.

'Do you want a hot chocolate?' Mum is asking. I roll my eyes. If only hot chocolate could fix it all. Mum suddenly seems to think so, it's her answer to everything. She seems afraid to say what everyone is thinking, afraid to ask those awkward questions.

'Are you sure you don't want to talk about it?'

Silence. Then I hear a sob from Beth.

'I'm fine,' she mutters but we know she's not. 'What happened to Sasha?' she asks.

Who's Sasha?

'I think she got married.'

The conversation ends there and I get bored so I

retreat to my bedroom. That chocolate bar will have to wait. It isn't long before I hear Beth tiptoeing up the stairs to her bedroom, afraid to be heard. I put her out of my mind and get out my Physics homework. I hate Physics. Whoever invented it should be shot. I struggle for five minutes trying to understand but to no avail.

*Have you done the physics hw?* I say in a text to Olivia.

*We have homework?*

*Great ty - big help*

*Sorry*

I put my phone down. I am about to text Katie when I remember that Beth is smart, she went to a grammar school. I take my book and burst a bit too forcefully into her room.

'Beth, do you know anything about Physics?'

Beth jumps. She looks terrified. She throws her phone down onto the bed as though it is a volcano about to erupt

'Sorry, did I interrupt something?'

'No it's fine.'

The word fine is starting to sound meaningless. She is obviously not fine.

'I did Physics at school … ten years ago.'

'Ah great. You can help me then.' I thrust my exercise book at her.

'I'm not convinced I will remember any of it.' However, she starts nodding. I'm glad someone gets it. It's a foreign language to me. Her explanations kind of make sense, way better than my Physics teacher. Pretty soon she has managed to explain it to me and, shock horror, I understand. She is good.

'Beth, you are a lifesaver,' I say, kissing her as I go to leave. She beams happily. I walk towards the door but then remember there is another part I don't understand.

'Oh and another thing- ' I stop when I see her phone buzzing next to her. Beth's eyes widen in terror as the name Michael flashes up.

'Who's Michael?'

‘No one,’ she answers somewhat unconvincingly.

‘Is he hassling you?’

‘Abby, leave it.’

‘I want to help.’

‘You don't know what you're getting into.’ Why does everyone think I am incapable of having intellectual thought?

‘Maybe you should explain it to me.’

‘I don’t want to,’ she replies forcibly.

‘Why can't you accept help?’ I’m starting to get annoyed now. ‘You're so selfish. When you left, you didn’t care about how it might affect us or how I might have felt, or that I missed you.’ I’m shouting but then I start crying at the same time.

‘It's not like that.’ All the fight has gone out of her.

‘No of course not.’ I slam the door on my way out.

Typical. She’s so full of her own problems. Doesn’t even give a thought to the rest of us who she left seven years ago. I wish for once she would tell me what’s going on. I’m not a small child anymore. A little voice in my head asks me if I could not have been more understanding.

*No I couldn’t have*, I answer. *She left us and now she won’t even let me help her.*

*Maybe you won’t be able to help.*

*But maybe I could try.*

‘Did I hear shouting?’ I hear Mum’s voice in Beth’s room. I roll my eyes to no one. Mum always has to get involved.

‘Abby and I had an argument.’

‘Anything I can do?’

‘No Mum, leave it.’ I almost laugh out loud, when has Mum ever left anything?

## January 4th 2018

I’m walking home after school and I see this weird man staring at me. He is tanned and muscly, standing behind one of the big oak trees, a good place to hide if you wanted to. The way he is looking at me is really creeping me out.

I've forgotten about him by the time I get home. Beth seems jumpy and pale faced when I let myself in. The TV is blaring out some late afternoon game show. Beth doesn't appear to be paying attention, just staring into space.

'You okay?' I ask cautiously. I don't want us to have an argument again.

She slides her phone under her pillow.

'Yeah.' But she's clearly not.

'Where's Mum?'

'Not back yet.'

'Please Beth, just tell me. I can see you're upset.'

'I can't,' she screams, tears flowing freely down her face. She rushes upstairs before I can question her further.

I want to help but I have no idea what's upsetting her. Part of me feels bad for shouting at her yesterday but part of me feels justified. The phone rings: it's Mum. I almost ignore it but I don't want to worry her. I grab it reluctantly, wondering why we still have a phone that's connected to the wall when everyone else has mobile ones.

'Abby, how are you both doing?'

'Fine.'

'And Beth?'

'Also fine. Why shouldn't we be?'

'No reason. Just had a strange message. Must be a wrong number.'

She hangs up without even saying goodbye, leaving me staring at the phone.

Recently I have wanted things to go back to the way they were before, but before what? Before Beth came back? Before Beth left in the first place? I don't know anymore. I'm so confused. I wish I had someone I could talk to, actually talk to. Someone who cared but wouldn't judge or interfere. Even my best friends are only in it for the drama. My life is chaotic right now.

I skulk slowly to the sofa to resume my daily position of *teenager watching bad TV shows after school.* First stop, change channel, get rid of the rubbish game show that's on there currently.

A noise from upstairs distracts me away from some dumb show on CBBC. Broken glass maybe? I run upstairs, expecting to see Beth clearing away a broken vase or something. I don't expect to see her cowering under her pink and purple covers, and a brick on the floor.

'Beth! What's happened?' None of it makes any sense until she points to a piece of paper on her bed.

*'Get back here or your family gets it.'*

'What is this?' I look out the window, not expecting to see anything. The street is quiet apart from the boy down the road on his bike.

Beth pulls down the cover, her complexion pale. 'Don't tell Mum and Dad,' she whispers.

'How can I not? They are going to see the broken window. Beth, this is serious. If someone is after you, us, we need to deal with this.'

'WE are not dealing with this - I am.'

'It doesn't seem like you can. Who is it? Who's after you? Is it Michael?'

'You don't understand.'

'Where does he want you to go back to?'

'You can't solve this.'

'Please, let me help you.'

Footsteps clomping up the stairs make us both stop. 'Please Abby,' she begs. I know she is asking me to support her lie. She grabs the note and chucks it down the side of her bed.

'Oh my gosh, what's happened to the window?' Mum exclaims.

'Some kid was messing around.'

'With a brick?! We need to call the police.'

'Mum, it's fine. I saw the person outside and they were

so frightened, they cycled away on their bike quickly. I didn't see much of him either.'

'Was it that boy down the road?'

'No!'

'Beth I can't let this go.'

'I'll pay for it. Don't worry.'

'Abby, did you see this?' They both look to me. I want to tell Mum the truth but how can I?

'No I didn't.' That much I don't have to lie about.

She shakes her head. 'What are kids like these days! Half of them are delinquents. Beth dear, we have to call the police.'

'No, please, Mum.'

Dad enters the room. Suddenly it feels very crowded in Beth's small room.

'What happened?'

'Some kids apparently,' says Mum. 'I want to call the police but Beth won't let me.' I expect Dad to back Mum up.

'She's right. Leave it. The police won't bother. Waste of time.'

He leaves before Mum can reply. She throws out a look of frustration at his distinct lack of support. Beth and I stare at each other but we stay silent.

She exits the room as quickly as she left it, calling out,

'I better phone some glaziers.'

'Thank you,' mouths Beth.

'This can't go on,' I answer back and go to leave her. Then a thought occurs to me. 'I saw a man earlier, standing under the tree, watching me.'

'What?' A horrified expression on her face. 'What did he look like?'

'Tanned, hot, but old.'

She suddenly looks very weak. 'Oh my god, it's him.'

Now I'm worried. Who is Michael? What does he want? Would he really hurt us?

**January 7th 2018**

I see her walking down the street; she thinks she is being subtle, getting away without any of us knowing. Where is she going, back pack in hand? Is she leaving again? That man, Michael, has something to do with this. I should run after her now but it's three am, I'm in my pyjamas and it's flipping freezing outside. Also, maybe a part of me wants her to go. Life is complicated with her around. This man could come after me. Does that sound selfish?

She walks quickly, glancing frantically.

Who knows who's lurking out there, waiting to *get* her. The thought of that man waiting for her makes me shudder. I need to tell them. I need to run after her but I don't move, my body stuck inside my warm cocoon of a bed.

Do it, I tell myself, but I don't. Mum wouldn't care that it's the middle of the night, she'd do anything for the prodigal daughter. I tell myself I'm helping Beth, giving her a head start. She's not stupid. I'm sure she's going somewhere safe. They'll find out soon enough.

Sleep is hard to come by after that. A million thoughts swirl round and round in my head. Half dreams where Beth is judging me angrily and Mum is crying over her lost child.

Early morning and I run downstairs and grab my phone before taking it up again. Mum is getting slack at spotting my early morning phone sessions.

*You awake?* I text Olivia.

*Yep kind of*

*You?*

*Um yes obviously*

*Oh yeah duh*

*Lol*

*What's up?*

*Beth's run away again.*

I don't tell her that I saw her go, that I could have

stopped her.

*Again*

*Why?*

*Something to do with this Michael man who keeps calling her*

*Do you think he's after her?*

*He might be*

*I bet your Mum's going crazy.*

*Yeah she is,* I lie.

I dread to think of how Mum will react to the news when she finds out. I wonder if Beth left a note or will we just have to figure it out? I'll have to tell Mum if not. I can't let her suffer not knowing.

I start to feel sleepy again and lay back on my pillow, putting my phone to one side. Maybe I'll try and get some more sleep.

~

'Jack, Jack.' I am woken by Mum shouting up the stairs at Dad. She knows. 'Jack, wake up!'

He mutters some response which I don't hear.

'Beth's gone!'

'What do you mean gone?' His voice louder now.

'She's run away again.'

'What? No. She can't be. Call the police.'

I am out in the hallway when Mum races downstairs.

'What's going on Mum?' She doesn't answer straight away, maybe thinking about telling me some lies, but then she laments.

'Beth's gone. She's run away.'

'It's my fault,' I mutter. She doesn't stop but rushes down.

I can hear her voice, loud and clear, frustrated. It doesn't seem like they are listening. I guess because she's an adult now it's not technically running away. Is this all too familiar for them? Is this what happened seven years ago? I need to tell them about Michael.

Dad and I are standing next to her when she has got off the phone.

'They are going to send someone round.'

We both nod. I sit down slowly and put my face in my hands. I should have stopped her. She's gone because I didn't help her. I knew about Michael and I did nothing. I feel ashamed.

'Abby, what did you mean when you said it was your fault?' Mum asks. Dad stares at me. I consider lying but Mum can always tell when I'm untruthful.

'I think there was someone after her.' Obviously I skip the part where I saw her leaving early this morning.

'Who?' demands Dad.

His sudden anger scares me but I have to tell them everything.

'She had a phone call from someone called Michael. She looked scared and didn't want to answer it. And that broken window- '

'Yes,' says Mum slowly.

'Someone threw a brick through the window with a note.'

'What? Why didn't you tell me?!' She is yelling at me now.

'I know. I know. I'm sorry.' I'm crying.

'What did the note say?' asks Dad.

'That she should get back there or her family would get it.'

'Get back where?' Mum's voice is getting more high-pitched with every revelation.

'I don't know.'

Then Mum stops as though she has remembered something 'I had a strange phone call at work the other day. A man said my girls were in danger.'

'That again. I told you before it was probably a prank call.' Dad seems so sure about that.

'But what if it wasn't.'

'Emily you read too much into things. We need to concentrate on finding Beth. Focusing on that call isn't helping. It's this Michael we need to be worrying about.'

Dad is looking increasingly distressed. 'Do you think she's gone back to him?'

'Not according to the letter she left us. She said she needs to get away to keep us safe.'

Mum hands the letter to Dad. He sits down and reads it. When he's finished he jumps up.

'I'm going to find her. I'm not letting her go again.' Wow, I can't believe my normally laid back Dad is so emotional, so decisive. 'You stay here. I'm getting dressed and going to try and track her down.'

'Can I come, Dad?' I ask.

'No, you stay with Mum. She needs you.' He runs off before anyone can argue with him. Mum grabs hold of me and pulls me into a hug like she doesn't ever want to let me go.

'Is this what happened last time?' I ask, my voice muffled through the jumper she is smothering me into. She pulls away.

'Kind of similar, yes. She went missing. We didn't get the text until two days later. We were going insane thinking she'd been kidnapped.'

'That's crazy, what did the text say?'

'That she'd gone away with a boyfriend. The police said they were trying to find her but it seemed like they had stopped trying.'

'Oh Mum. It must have been awful.'

'It was. It is.'

'Do you think Michael is the boyfriend?'

'I don't know. If he is then he's been manipulating her for a long time.'

**January 8th 2018**

I can't believe Mum is making me go to school with all this going on. It's all over the news now. Beth is being described as a vulnerable young adult, vulnerable because of the danger she's in. A man is wanted for questioning in connection with it. They think this man has made her leave again, that her note is a fake note meant to keep us happy. Is it Michael?

I have learnt more about my life in one day than I have in fifteen years. Little details about my parents' lives that I never knew before, such as that Mum used be a local councillor. Why has she never mentioned that to us? I learnt that Dad had a brother who died when he was five.

Now I am wondering if I ever really knew my family. Everyone has a different theory on who the man is but it is clear that none of them know anything, just random people venting on social media.

At school I can feel the stares as I enter the school grounds. I can hear the whispered tones. I am a precious doll that no one wants to touch. My friends crowd round me as if I am a celebrity.

'Are you okay?'

'It must be so scary.'

'Has she been kidnapped do you think?'

'Who's that man they are talking about?'

'Did you actually get a brick thrown through the window?'

The questions are endless and I am beginning to wish I had fought harder to stay at home though that's not a great option either. I know Mum will be pacing the house furiously. Either way I am helpless to do anything.

'Sorry guys, I don't want to talk about it.'

I can see my 'friends' are disappointed. They just want to dissect my life but the newspapers have already done that.

The teachers take it easy on me. I am distracted, I am slow, I am dreamy - the things I usually get told off for, but today they don't say a word. Today I have a good reason.

Images of the monster that is Michael fill my head and won't leave. In my mind he is the brute from beauty and the beast. I am scared for Beth. Will she be trapped forever and then fall in love with him until our Dad agrees to pay up? I know how it works.

Then there is the guilt that is eating away at my insides. I should have said something earlier. I should have told Mum that Michael was ringing her, but would it have made any difference if I had?

'Abby are you okay?' The rest of the class has gone. The end of the lesson has come and gone. I find myself staring up into Mr Gordon's big blue eyes, not an entirely unpleasant sight.

'Sorry, I didn't realise it was time to go.'

'It's okay. You obviously have a lot on your mind. Do you want to talk about it?'

I shrug. 'Maybe.'

'I guess you must be worried about your sister.'

My eyes start to water before I can stop them. I brush them away furiously and turn away. I can't believe I am crying in front of Mr Gordon. 'Sorry,' I mutter.

'You don't have to be sorry.'

'It's my fault,' I cry out.

'Oh Abby, this is not your fault.'

'I should have told them what I knew.'

'Even if you had it might not have stopped your sister going off again. She sounds a pretty determined girl.'

I smile a little. 'I guess she is.' I get up, embarrassed at the scene I have made of myself. 'I should go and get some lunch.'

'I'm here if you need to talk.' His kindness makes me want to cry even more. I fight back the tears as I smile at him and leave the classroom quickly. Luckily the corridors are virtually empty as I scurry away to find a toilet to make myself look half decent. Katie is already in the bathroom staring at herself in the mirror.

'Are you okay, you look awful?'

'Aw thanks.'

'Sorry. I didn't mean it like that.'

'It's fine … it's just hard at the moment.'

'I can't imagine how you must be feeling.' She sounds like a carefully scripted counsellor. She must have been watching some stupid American show.

'No you can't.' I feel angry but instantly regret taking it out on her. 'Sorry,' I add. She smiles and puts her arm around me. I don't deserve such a good friend.

The school day draws to an agonising close. I considered texting Mum several times during the day but couldn't bring myself to. Partly because I am worried that it will be bad news and partly because I am worried there will be no news. I don't know what's worse.

Mum is sitting at the breakfast bar in the kitchen, head in her hands. When she looks up it is as if wrinkles have appeared on her face. Uncle Pete is there making them coffee.

'Any news?' I ask hopefully, already knowing the answer.

'No.' Uncle Pete comes over and puts his arm around me, squeezing me close to him.

'They'll find her.' I'm not convinced by his optimism and wriggle free from his embrace.

'Is Dad still out looking?' I say turning to Mum.

'I think so, and the police. He said he'd text with news but he hasn't.'

I sit on the stool next to her and link my arm with hers. I wonder if life will always be a constant rollercoaster of Beth leaving and Beth returning.

## January 13th 2018

I've never seen Mum like this, so helpless, so frantic as she paces up and down the lounge like a caged animal. It is Saturday and no school. If I thought being at school was bad, trying to concentrate with all this going on is a hundred times worse. Mum has turned into this stress monster and I don't know what to do.

I've no idea how but Dad managed to figure out that

Beth has gone to Norwich. Not sure where Norwich is or how big it is but I think it's a city. Finding a girl who wants to be lost in a big city is not going to be easy. Several times since she left again I have cursed myself for not stopping her, for not running after her or for not telling Mum and Dad so they could go after her. Just because I couldn't be bothered to get out of my warm bed.

'Mum, it'll be okay.' She doesn't look convinced and I don't feel certain. She checks her phone for what seems like the thousandth time. 'Anything?' She shakes her head.

I don't know how to deal with her. She is supposed to be the one in control, the one consoling me, the one who always knows what to do.

Her phone pings. She grabs it, almost falling over in the process.

'Dad says he's not found her yet.' She puts the phone down, hands shaking.

She goes back to pacing but this time she is muttering. 'I can't do this. Please don't let her be gone again.' Her muttering turns to shouting. This is the part in films where someone would rush in with a tranquiliser gun. '*She can't cope, she needs Valium.*'

'Mum, Mum you have to calm down.' I try the rub her arm approach. No you guessed it, doesn't work very well. Never worked on me when she did it either. 'You can't fall apart. Beth needs you.' I want to add *I need you.* She looks at me as if she is seeing me for the first time.

'You're right. I'm sorry. I'm a mess.' I should say she's not but she really is. 'It's just it's so hard. I can't sleep. I can't think straight.'

'I know, I know.' I don't know, but that's what you say. I know how I feel but Mum seems to feel this extra stuff like guilt. Where on earth does she get the idea that it's her fault? She's always loved Beth, it's clear to see. No one would ever accuse her of being a bad Mum, not in that way.

'When Beth left seven years ago it was awful.' I know, I

was there. Okay, I was eight but I was still upset. 'I thought she was dead. I can't do this again. I can't let her go.'

I don't think she's ever let her go. It's clear to me now that Mum has always been on edge and this has thrown her over once more and now she's clinging on for dear life. I only hope I can catch her. My phone pings. We both jump. It's only Olivia.

*hey*

*how's it going?*

Her cheerful tone reminds me that there is an outside world, not one I'm part of right now.

'It's Olivia,' I explain. Disappointed, Mum goes back to pacing the room.

*Not so good right now Beth's still gone*

*Still?? No way*

*Sorry*

*What are you going to do*

*Dads out looking for her*

*Hope he finds her*

*Its crazy mums going mad*

*Do you wanna come over here? We can watch Netflix:)*

More than anything I'd love to escape to Olivia's house right now. Netflix would be a great distraction but I need to be here. I'm afraid of what Mum might do if I go out.

*I can't leave mum she needs me she's literally falling apart.*

*Let me know if you change your mind*

'How about we go for a walk?' I suggest, anything to get her out of this house. The atmosphere is starting to stifle us both. She looks horrified at the suggestion.

'I can't leave. She might come home.'

'But we know she's in Norwich. She's unlikely to be home yet. A quick walk round the block. It won't take long and the fresh air will do you good. Isn't that what you're always telling me?'

She smiles at her own argument being used against her. It does sound strange coming out of my mouth. I'm turning into an old woman.

'A very quick walk.'

Pleased with my success, I drag her out of the door before she can change her mind. Who would have believed I would be the one suggesting we go for a walk? We don't talk as we march down the road, my arm in hers. I'm finding it difficult to keep up, she desperately wants to get back but already I can see her face is brighter and more hopeful.

'I'm sure Dad will find her,' I lie. I don't think that but I say it because it's what she wants to hear. She smiles and squeezes my arm. I'm not sure she believes me either.

Up the road we meet a neighbour, an old lady from two doors away. She often chats to Mum but I haven't spoken to her for years except for her commenting on how big I'm getting.

'Ooh, I hear your daughter's back.' There is a naughty glint in her eye. If she were a baddie in a film she would be rubbing her hands together in glee and cackling loudly.

'Um yes,' answers Mum.

'How exciting for you. Did she say where she's been all this time?'

'We are talking about it yes.' Mum is cagey and I don't blame her. How dare this woman march up and demand to know these things just because she likes a bit of a gossip. She should get back to her gardening.

'Did she get up to anything adventurous?'

'We're not up for talking right now,' I say rudely. 'We've got to get back.' I pull Mum away before I say anything I'll regret. Mum giggles.

'You didn't need to be quite so rude,' she chuckles.

'Me, rude? She was so nosy.'

'She's obviously not got much else to talk about.'

'Well, she should go on Facebook then, get a life.'

'Haha can you imagine her on Facebook.' I do imagine it and all I can picture is photos of her gardens, her brightly coloured flowers and the soup she makes or whatever else old people do. That's if she could even figure out how to use it and I doubt that she could.

'Quite a few old people use Facebook,' says Mum.

'Oh you mean like that old guy you know who posts random pictures of historic lamp posts or objects? How on earth does he get so many likes for them?'

We laugh and it feels good to have a distraction even if only for a short time. When we get back home I am filled with hope. We will get through this, we have to.

## January 14th 2018

Another night's sleep and still no news of Beth. I slept in Mum's bed last night. I really am regressing to being a five-year-old now. I don't know who needed the comfort more, her or me. We stayed up and watched a film, anything to keep our minds off her. I felt her tossing and turning, affecting my sleep too. The sooner she is found the better so we can get on with our lives again. I've been ignoring the fact that even if she does return, the problem of Michael remains.

That makes me afraid.

I have no idea who Michael is or why he's even after Beth. I wish she had talked to me. Whatever it is that she thinks - I'm too young to understand or handle - she's wrong. Not knowing is worse. I am now imagining all sorts of bad things, probably none of them even close to the truth. Judging from Mum's tired expression and worry lines she is probably going through the same thought processes.

I make Mum breakfast in bed, knowing she probably won't eat it, but at least I feel I have done my duty. She is sitting up, on her phone, when I return. I don't want to ask if there is any news, she would have told me if there was.

'No news,' she says glumly.

'Maybe later,' I say hopefully.

I switch on the TV in Mum and Dad's room. I can't

remember the last time I did that, cuddled up with her in bed. It used to be a typical Saturday morning event, one I would look forward to. I am sure the wall paper in this room was once was in fashion. It doesn't match with the rest of the house but then it's not a place Mum spends much time in.

There's not much to watch on TV on a Sunday morning except cooking shows so we end up watching one of those. I watch them lay some gross fish thing on the plate with a bit of salad, triumphant over their masterpiece. Surely no one would eat that? Not only is it small and barely fills the plate but where are the potatoes or something to go with it? I am pondering this very thought when Mum's phone pings with a message. She picks it up and her face quickly goes from despondent to happy.

'Dad says he's found Beth and he's bringing her home.'

'Really?' I am amazed. I can't believe he found her and actually managed to persuade her to come back. I watch Mum send Dad a barrage of emojis and call him a hero. Something about her response makes me feel uncomfortable. She starts crying.

'What's wrong?'

'I'm so relieved.' Parents are weird sometimes. Imagine crying about something good.

With a new energy Mum jumps out of bed, pulling on her jeans and jumper from a nearby chair. She's making me tired looking at her.

'I've got to get stuff ready.' What does she have to get ready? It's not like the queen is coming to tea. She races downstairs and soon I can hear the hoover going. I suppose I better get dressed too.

Mum cleans the house thoroughly. You would think that royalty is coming to stay. I try to position myself on the sofa in my usual viewing seat but the hoovering and constant cleaning is getting in the way of it. She finally finishes and sits down next to me, exhausted.

When Beth and Dad arrive home a few hours later, he

is parading her around, with a massive grin, he's the hero of the day. Whereas the bags under Beth's eyes tell a different story. Mum veers from hugging Beth continuously to saying how wonderful Dad is. It's enough to make anyone throw up. Beth smiles slightly at me. I detect a hint of embarrassment. She sits down on the sofa while Mum and Dad disappear into the kitchen, to bask in his glory.

'Hi,' I say shyly. 'Are you okay?'

She shrugs. 'Not sure. I'm glad to be home.'

'You can talk to me you know,' I offer.

She sighs deeply, as though it's been held in for a while. 'I know. I just don't want to burden you with it.'

'What are you worried about?'

'About Michael.'

'What about him?'

'That he'll come get us.'

'I'm sure Dad will protect us,' I say trying to reassure her though I'm not convinced myself. He may have found her in Norwich but is he a match for Michael?

'Yeah you're probably right. I'm sorry if I didn't tell you about him. I only wanted to protect you.'

'Thanks. I know that. I want to help. I may not be as street wise as you but I'm not stupid.'

'I know.'

'So what did you do in Norwich? Where did you stay? And why Norwich?'

'Because I went to the train station and that was where the next train was going to. I'd heard it was a cool place. I crashed at some dodgy people's houses and tried to get a job.'

'It sounds- ' I don't want to say boring but I'm thinking it.

'It felt good to be away from the stress but the place I was living was awful.'

'I'm glad Dad came and rescued you then.'

'I'm glad too,' says Dad coming into the room followed

by Mum.

'Was it really terrible there?' asks Mum anxiously.

'No it was fine,' Beth answers quickly.

'So how did you find her in such a big city?' I ask Dad. He looks awkward but then hides it quickly.

'Because I'm a genius at finding people I guess,' he laughs loudly. I suspect it was a collaborative effort from him and the police but I'll let him have his glory.

'Well let's get sat down. I've made us a roast dinner,' announces Mum.

**January 15th 2018**

I see him before anyone else does, the same man as before. Casually leaning against a tree with a provocative look on his face. I'm sure it's Michael. I can see why she was attracted to him if it is. He makes you feel special, the way his eyes take in your whole body, his confident stance that tells me he knows what he wants. While everyone else is playing happy reunions they forgot about the dangers. He puts his finger to his lips and then pretends to slash his throat, with a slight smile on his face. Then he flicks his hair off his face, flirting with every movement. I know it is a threat but secrets got Beth nowhere. I don't know why I don't mention it while we are there near him but I am afraid. Mum and Dad and Beth are ahead of me; he must have just emerged. He's not stupid.

'I saw him,' I blurt out, as soon as we are safe inside. Beth's eyes widen in fear. Mum clutches Dad's hand.

'Where?'

'At the end of the road. He threatened me.'

'Oh my- ' exclaims Mum, panic already filling her eyes.

'This is going to stop.' He opens the front door with such force that it hits the wall leaving a tiny dent.

'Wait, what are you doing?' Beth shouts.

Fear grips hold of me.

'I'm going to talk to this guy.'

'But you don't know what he's capable of.' It's too late. Dad is already halfway down the street. What is he capable of? Did he ever hurt Beth?

'Go back inside.' Mum ushers us in and shuts the door. We wait in the hallway, none of us say a word. I kick my shoes off but then regret it as I stand on the cold tiled floor. I think about getting my slippers but am frozen in the moment. I don't want to miss a thing; I can't afford to miss a thing. Within minutes Dad is back.

'What happened?' asks Mum before he can speak.

'He was gone. I'm calling the police.' No one argues with him.

~

The policewoman is writing furiously, excited by the prospect of something other than a standard missing teenager case, while Beth recounts details about Michael and friends.

The other police officer, younger and appearing to be less stressed, is sitting beside her, smiling occasionally. I am perched on the edge of Dad's armchair, making me feel like I am not that important. For one surreal moment I am looking down on this and wondering how on earth our lives got to be so messed up. I should be excited by the prospect of police officers in our house - my friends would have a field day if they knew - but now it's serious. It's not exciting. Our lives are in danger.

Mum wants to protect me, for me to go upstairs, but I'm not a baby anymore. Dad agrees to let me stay, thinking that if I know the truth it may help me stay safe. I'm not sure anymore but I'm glad I'm not being shut out. Beth tells them how she was taken in by Michael, how he loved her. Who wouldn't fall for an attractive older man? *It was the pressure of grammar school, she needed a break from it* Mum turns away guiltily. I always wondered why they never pushed me much at school, now I know.

'So Michael is big, and tanned you say?' The police officer asks looking up from her notepad.

'Yes, I guess I thought he was … well, cute looking.' She looks embarrassed. I feel her pain. I totally would be too in front of Mum and Dad. Beth's account of how she met Michael makes sense, the flattering messages on the chatroom, their first meeting at the shopping centre. Though I struggle to understand why he would want to meet there. Surely he would have more class than to buy clothes at our local mall that has seen more shops close in the past year than ever, especially when Lakeside is not that far away? I know where I would choose to go.

'So seven years ago, you ran away to move in with him?'

'That's right.'

'Did he make you run away?' Dad's face is looking thunderous.

'No.'

'How did he come across to you when you first moved in with him?'

'He was sweet. He seemed to genuinely care about me. He said he loved me.' Dad makes a noise. Beth glares at him.

'Did he pressurise you into having sex?' The abrupt tone of her questioning shocks me, Mum wriggles in her seat. The other officer raises his eyebrows. I can sense a giggle emerging in me, I don't know why. I push it down and force myself to focus.

'No. He said we'd do it when I was ready.'

'And did that moment happen?'

Beth looks away before answering. 'Yes about a month after I'd moved in we were cuddling in bed and one thing led to another. You know?'

I'm not sure the fifty year old policewoman does know but she nods anyway.

'Bloody hell,' whispers Dad. I think Mum is going to cry. 'Shouldn't you be out there trying to find this guy?' Dad cries impatiently.

'Don't worry Mr Kimmings we already have people out

there looking but it is important for us to gather as much information about him and his friends as possible so we can get a fuller picture.'

Her speech sounds rehearsed, like it's something she says to every victim.

Mum touches his arm as if to tell him to back off a bit. The other officer looks sympathetically at Dad.

'Believe me, I know this is hard,' he insists. 'If it were my daughter I'd want to deck the guy but you have to trust us and let us do our job.' He barely looks old enough to be a dad. How would he know what it's like? Dad gets up, switching the kettle on when he reaches the kitchen.

'So Beth,' the first police officer turns to her again. 'When did it start to go wrong?'

She sighs. It is a big question and not one that is going to be answered quickly. I settle down into the sofa. This may take a while.

# Part Two

## Beth - Seven Years Earlier

### December 1st 2010

*'You're so pretty', his first message said to me. I wanted someone to love me. 'Wouldn't you like an older man as your boyfriend?' It was as if he could read my mind. 'Do you want to meet? I'll meet you anywhere as long as I can have you in my arms.' So romantic, I needed that.*

'Hi there, you waiting for someone?' I laugh nervously, this must be him. *Look out for the tall dark handsome stranger with a pink flower in his hand.* He hands me the rose with a soft smile.

'It's good to meet you,' I say, knowing that I sound like an idiot. A cute man talking to me. He's different though, not like the boys in my year. He's obviously older but not by much. Tanned with gorgeous dark eyes. Already I am mesmorised.

'I promised you I would take you for a coffee.'

I don't even drink coffee and I can't believe he actually wants to hang out with me. Sasha will be so jealous when she meets him.

'Yeah, why not,' I reply casually but inside I am an excited little kid.

He takes me to a posh little cafe on the high street, not a place I would usually go or even knew existed. I order a coffee because I don't want him to think I am a child. Maybe he imagines I am older anyway. He can't know that I'm only fifteen.

'It's so good to finally meet you.' He has no idea. 'How's your friend?'

'Sasha?'

'Yeah, you said you'd had some kind of an argument.'

'We did, kind of, it was nothing. She doesn't understand me sometimes.'

'Friends can be like that.'

'She's constantly standing me up. She's a bit wild and unpredictable but I guess that's why I enjoy hanging out with her.' He is staring intently at me. He brushes the hair that has fallen over his face away and smiles. He seems to be genuinely interested in what I have to say. The same way he has always been.

'You said you're a salesman, what do you sell?'

'Oh you don't want to talk about that. It's boring stuff.' I don't want to talk about it either. I was just being polite. 'How about you? How's college?'

'It's great,' I lie. On the chatroom I told him I was doing A levels; English, Philosophy and Physics. I only hope he doesn't test me on them.

'I like a girl who has ambition.' The way he says it sends shivers down my spine. Did he just say he likes me? I could pinch myself, this can't be real. I must be having some kind of a dream.

After we have chatted for over an hour, he tells me he has to be somewhere. He promises to text me again. I walk away, hoping he will stay good to his promise, but what if he doesn't? What if, now he's met me, I'm a disappointment. What would a guy like him see in little old me? I am halfway down the street when my phone pings.

*Loved meeting you today. Would like to see you again. Maybe we could do this again next Saturday?*

*But only if you want to*

He messaged me, he actually messaged me! He likes me. I can't believe it! I am so excited! How do I reply? I don't want to seem too keen. So I respond with:

*That would be lovely. I can't wait.*

~

'You look happy.' Mum is staring at me creepily.

'Um, maybe I am,' I answer slowly, sneaking upstairs before she can ask me any more questions. I don't want to talk about it with her. I don't need her judgement.

Abby bursts into my room minutes later. 'Beth, Beth, can you play the bus stop game with me?' All I want to do is lay on my bed and dream of Michael but I say yes. I can't refuse that sweet little face.

'Just for a little bit as I've got homework to do,' I lie.

She runs excitedly into her room to get it. When she returns, she lays it out on the floor, connecting the board piece by piece.

I was kind of hoping she'd got fed up with this game by now. It's tedious, she cheats and it's way below her age range. And if you try to call her out she runs to Mum who always takes Abby's side. *She's only eight.* Apparently being an eight year old means you can't lose at anything. I'm pretty sure I always lost at games to Dad at her age and I didn't cry about it.

'I'm red, you're going to be blue.' That's the other thing that annoys me, what if I don't want to be blue. I don't care that much but I would like a choice.

She puts the counters at the beginning of the bus route and rolls the dice. It lands on a one.

'Wait, that wasn't a proper roll,' she exclaims and rolls it again. I've given up arguing with her on these matters. Finally she gets six after about three attempts but as she moves forward she realises she is about to land on a bad square, the one where you have to take away passengers on your bus. She screws up her face, I quickly grab the dice and take my go before she can claim it didn't say six in the first place. I roll a five and land on an add passengers square. Five passengers for me.

'What's that on your arm?'

'Nothing,' I say quickly, pulling down my sleeve to hide the marks. I thought they'd faded but clearly not enough.

As she rolls the dice for her second go, my phone rings next to me. It's Michael. I pick it up, torn between answering it too quick and losing him due to not answering it quick enough. Finally I click on the green button, hands shaking.

'Hi.'

'Hi babe. How you doing?'

'Um … fine.' Eurgh, I sound like an idiot.

'I miss you already. I can't wait for our next date.' Did he say date? Wow, he actually misses me.

'Um … I miss you too,' I say, unsure of whether I should say that or not but he responds positively.

'Your go,' announces Abby loudly.

'Who's that?'

'Oh, just my little sister.' I put my finger on my lips to indicate that Abby should be quiet. She does not look happy.

'I bet she's cute.'

'Yeah, sometimes.' He laughs.

'Beth, it's your go.' This time louder and more insistent.

'Yes okay,' I whisper urgently. 'Just wait.'

'I better leave you to it. It sounds like your sister needs you.' I want to tell him that she can wait but I don't want to be that horrible person. 'I'll call you again.'

'That would be great.'

When he has hung up, I turn to Abby angrily.

'I was on the phone and that was very rude. You need to be more patient.'

'He's rude.'

'There are more important things than your stupid game.'

'It's not a stupid game!'

I sigh. I can see the beginnings of a tantrum so I retreat before it gets bad.

'Okay it's not stupid but it was an important phone call.'

'Was it your boyfriend?'

'None of your business.' She giggles.

I am about to shout at Abby when my phone lights up. *Missing you already*,

'Beth's got a boyfriend,' she chants.

'Shush. I don't want everyone knowing.'

'Why not?'

'Just because. It's our little secret. Promise you won't tell Mum.'

'Pinky promise,' She holds out her little finger to mine. I take it and smile. I only hope she can keep secrets.

I've already been hiding this secret for months, Mum walking in the room when I'm reading his messages, her asking me what I'm doing, why I'm always glued to that thing. I can't tell her it's all because of him.

Our next date is ten times more special. Michael takes me to a lovely cafe out of town, the kind me and my friends wouldn't go near. He asks me so many questions about my life, he really seems to care about me. I can tell Sasha is dead jealous when I tell her about him on Monday.

'So how old is he?'

'No idea, probably about twenty.'

'And handsome?'

'Um yeah, course.'

'You're so lucky. I wish I had an older man after me.'

I beam, feeling as though I am the luckiest girl alive. I dodge the question of where we met. She doesn't need to know that.

## December 13th 2010

'You off out again?' I continue brushing my hair in the mirror, ignoring Mum. 'You've got school tomorrow.'

'It's all good, stop stressing.'

'Your exams are soon.'

'After Christmas, Mum, not yet.' I know my voice is starting to start patronising but she is really annoying me now.

'You can't let it slip. You've got to- '

'I know, get those grades.' It's all anyone goes on about. I sometimes wish I had been stupid, not smart, at least then I could fail in peace.

'You want to do A levels.'

*She* wants me to do A levels. I'm not sure I have a choice in the matter.

'It'll be fine. We're only going to the cinema.' A white lie.

'You and Sasha?'

'Yes.' Another white lie.

'Promise me you'll knuckle down over Christmas.'

'Yes, yes, I will.' I'll say anything to get her off my back but if I'm hoping she'll go away, I am wrong.

'Are you going out like that?' She stares down at my short black dress disapprovingly.

'Oh for goodness sake, I'm just going to the cinema.'

'But why do you need to dress up like that?'

'I'm fifteen,' I yell. 'I can wear what I want.'

'Fifteen is not that old.'

My fists clench around the hair brush, furiously drawing it through my hair.

'I'll see you later.' I throw the hairbrush on the floor and run down the stairs before she can stop me.

'Beth, we need to talk.'

I slam the door before she can add anything further.

## December 14th 2010

Pretty soon a few dates have developed into a relationship. Even after he discovers I am only fifteen he still wants to see me. I was so worried that it would put him off but he was so sweet about it. Michael thinks it would be more special if we keep it to ourselves. I don't tell him that I've already told Sasha. I don't want to make him mad.

'Hey babe, why don't you come and live with me?'

'What, you mean permanently? Now?'

'Yeah, why not?'

The thought makes me uneasy yet it's so exciting at the

same time, to be an adult living away from home, with an older man. When I mention school, he replies: 'You don't need school. I'll look after you.'

It is too tempting, especially after the argument with Mum yesterday.

'What will I tell Mum and Dad?'

He sighs.

'I'm sure you can decide that.'

I can't though. How do I tell them I want to move out and live with an older man? There's no way they would agree to that. There is another possibility: I could run away. The more I think of it the more it seems a real option.

**December 18th 2010**

So, a week before Christmas I pack my bags and go. I say goodbye to Mum in the morning as I leave for school in my uniform but change out of it as soon as I can. I don't want him thinking I'm just a school girl anymore. I think about leaving Mum and Dad a note but I don't. I'll text them in a few days. They might have calmed down by then. I kiss Abby goodbye and feel a teensy bit guilty. Who will she have to beat at the bus stop game?

Michael is waiting in town as arranged when I get there, his face full of smiles. I can't believe this is happening. I am moving in with my boyfriend for real. He kisses me on the cheek and takes my bag off me before leading me to his car and my new life.

**December 19th 2010**

Oh my gosh, my life is so exciting right now. Today I should be sitting through endless lessons at school, with teachers going on and on about the exams after Christmas.

Instead of Science, I am sitting in Michael's apartment eating his fancy breakfast. Okay, maybe I hate special K but I am not going to admit that. He thinks I'm mature. I have to keep it up.

Last night I slept in his bed. He insisted on sleeping on the sofa until I got settled. What a gentleman. His apartment is so modern with kitchen surfaces that glitter and shine and all the latest gadgets. He has the most amazing coffee machine I've ever seen.

The journey to get here seemed endless, probably only an hour away, but farther than I'd imagined.

'How did you sleep?' he asks, peering round the bedroom door.

'Good,' I answer nervously. I don't know why but I feel shy around him now. Back when I first met him I was blown away by his gorgeous smile, we chatted like we'd known each other forever. I couldn't believe he'd look at me twice.

I reach out to grab my phone.

'Strange. It won't switch on.' Michael shrugs at me. 'What's up with this thing.' I tap it roughly a few times, take the back off, but nothing helps.

'No idea. Maybe you should get a new one anyway. That one's a bit old.'

'I'd love a new one but I've got no money.'

'I'll buy you one. Early Christmas present.'

'I can't let you do that. That's far too expensive,'

'Hey don't worry about that. I can afford it and besides you're worth it.'

How amazing is that, a man buying me a phone. Why does it feel so wrong though?

'I've got to go out and meet some friends. Are you gonna be alright here on your own?'

I nod, a little disappointed. I had hoped we would spend the day together, watch a movie maybe, cuddle, you know, that kind of thing.

As he leaves, I wonder what kind of friends he is meeting that he needs to wear a smart suit. The boys at school wouldn't dream of wearing a shirt unless it had some kind of dumb logo on it. They are so immature.

I spend the morning watching endless American soaps on Sky until I am bored. Dad would never let us get Sky, says it's a waste of money and only people with too much would get it. I decide to go for a walk and put my coat on but at that moment Michael arrives home.

'Going somewhere?'

'I was going for a walk. Getting lonely here on my own.'

He takes my coat off me. 'You don't need to now. I'm home.' I don't argue, I let him take it as I sit down again.

'Did you have a good time with your friends?'

'Oh yes,' he answers in a tone I can't quite understand. 'So, tonight I am taking you out for dinner.'

“Ooh, sounds good.' I am expecting Pizza Hut or Frankie and Benny’s or some other chain type restaurant.

'Marchello’s,' he says, looking at me to be impressed.

'Isn't that expensive?'

'Babe, you are worth it.'

But I don't have any posh clothes to wear.'

'It’s not a problem, I bought you some dresses while I was out.' He waves a plastic bag at me. I grab it excitedly. A guy buying me clothes, could you get any more exciting or perfect than that? I pull out the first dress, a red shiny straight number, like something a model would wear. The second is blue, long and made of chiffon. At the bottom are some tights. He has thought of everything.

'I'll wear this one tonight,’ I say, holding up the red dress.

'Good choice.' He pulls me to him in a cuddle, chucking the dress on the sofa. 'You're going to look amazing.' The way his hands slide down my back and gently squeezes my bottom sends shivers of excitement down my spine.

'I'll make us lunch.' He draws away from me leaving me wanting more, much more.

Lunch is a disappointing salad. I don't want to say

anything but the disappointment must show on my face as he adds 'I know it's not much but you want to keep your figure gorgeous.' I agree and am glad he is thinking of me, so thoughtful.

Every now and then during lunch he smiles at me with that sweet smile. I can't wait for our dinner tonight. Leaving home was not a hard decision. The stifling pressure I felt at that school, at home, was too much. I need to be somewhere where I can be free.

I stand in front of the mirror in the red dress, black silky tights on and my hair curled. I feel amazing. If my friends at school could see me now. I could easily pass for someone in their twenties. I carefully put on the lipstick, the only one I brought with me, fortunately in red. Michael sneaks up behind me. I smile as he puts his arms around me. His fingers trace the faint lines on my arm.

'Stunning! You look gorgeous. Absolutely scrumptious.' His hands slide all over me as his eyes give me the once over. 'Come on, let's go. Don't want to be late.' I am glad to get out after having spent the day in his apartment. As nice as it is, I missed getting fresh air. Michael drives us in his Lexus - Dad would be impressed by it. I wonder if Dad would like Michael. He likes men with style.

*Marchello's* is every bit as posh as I'd imagined. Even the waiters are dressed in black suits and bow ties. The place is buzzing and I can see all kinds of weird and wonderful food on people's plates. I worry for a moment that I won't be able to find anything I like but I'm so hungry that I could eat anything. Special K and salad is not much to keep you going.

Michael bypasses the queue and says something to the waiter that I don't quite hear. He smiles at us and picks up four menus, I look around wondering why. I am disappointed when we are shown to a table that already has two men sitting there. They both stand up when they see us. I had hoped it would be the two of us. Their beaming smiles are enough to make me feel welcome though.

'You must be Beth. I'm Jeremy,' says the first man with his hand stretched out to shake mine.

I smile at him shyly. The second one, a very tall muscular man, grabs my other hand and kisses it.

'Stuart. You are as gorgeous as we'd heard.'

They are very charming, asking me lots of questions, so attentive. I have never felt so wanted by anyone. I notice they avoid asking me anything about school. I'm glad, I don't want to be reminded that I am only fifteen. I'm finally being treated like a grown up. I order a steak from the menu as it's the only thing I can work out what it is but instantly worry that it is not lady-like enough. Fortunately Michael doesn't seem to react. When the food arrives I am so hungry that I immediately start tucking in at great speed. Michael shoots me a disapproving look, making me realise I am being rude. I slow down and he smiles at me. I don't want to upset him.

### December 21st 2010

Three days in and I suddenly remember I was supposed to text Mum. Oops. I hope she's not mad about it. When I mention it to Michael he's not keen. My new phone hasn't arrived yet so he lends me one of his, a small cheap looking thing. No idea why he would have one like this. I don't even know how it works.

After I have figured out how to text on it, I message Mum.

*Hi Mum just to let you know I've moved in with a boyfriend.*

I get an instant reply *Where are you? We thought you'd been kidnapped. I've been going insane.*

I didn't even think about that, but kidnapped - really? I can handle myself. Besides, I'm not a kid anymore, no one kidnaps a fifteen year old.

*I'm fine stop worrying.*

She doesn't reply but rings me. Oh crap I do not want

to talk to her. Cancelling the call, I switch off the phone. Michael takes it away.

'You don't need this anymore.' He disappears into the bedroom with it. When he returns, a few minutes later, he studies my face. 'You good, babe?' Michael's use of the word babe, while sweet to begin with, is starting to grate on me a little.

'Yeah, why wouldn't I be?'

'You seem a little upset that's all.'

'It's fine.'

He can't know how I feel. He'd think I was some kind of baby. I can't shake the feeling that I've done something wrong. I hate to think of Mum worrying but she knows I'm okay.

Mum would never have run away. She's far too goody two shoes for that. She doesn't understand. She tries to be cool but she doesn't manage it. Mum's can't be cool.

He sits down on his sofa and pats the seat next to him. There's something so grown up about this sofa, it's soft, you could sink into it and never get up

Michael switches on the TV and the news is on with a story about a missing teenager. At first I think it's about me and hold my breath, hoping that my pale face and wide eyes don't betray my feelings.

Fortunately it's about another fifteen year old who went missing two days ago. Her Mum is pleading with us, anguish in her face, willing us to tell her anything we know. It makes me feel uncomfortable. The tired expression and washed out face suggests she hasn't slept in days. Does Mum feel like this? Surely not. This is different of course, I'm not missing. I'm not technically a runaway either. I moved in with my boyfriend. Totally different situation. I wonder if Mum will call Sasha's Mum. Thank goodness I didn't tell her anything. I was desperate to but I knew she would tell the second she could.

Michael changes channel rapidly, clearly he is disturbed by the pleading mother too. He settles on an action film.

It's not one I would have chosen but I go along with it.

I find it hard to concentrate, I can't stop thinking about Mum.

'What's up?'

'Mum. I'm wondering if I should call her back.' He wrinkles his nose in disgust, making me feel like a little kid who should know better.

'No I wouldn't. She'll get over it eventually. You're a big girl now. What good would it do calling her? She'd only make you feel bad.'

He's right, I know he is, but it's so hard. I hate that I am making my Mum suffer but there is no way I want to go home. I love Michael. I love being here. For the first time ever I am not controlled by an overbearing mother, not pressured by a school because I am not getting the "A"s that I am apparently capable of. Who cares? There is more to life than grades and I am living life, living it gloriously right now.

'Yeah, you're right.'

'I almost forgot,' Michael murmurs, pulling something out of his pocket, a packet.

'What's that?'

'The pill. Just in case, you know-' His face reddens.

'Oh right, yes.'

'I didn't want to be presumptuous but-'

'No, you're right. I don't want to get pregnant.'

I take the packet of pills, hiding it away in my pocket and snuggle into Michael's warm and manly chest. How lucky am I to have a man who thinks of everything. Soon all thoughts of Mum disappear from my mind as he distracts me. We cuddle, nothing else. He's so good, no pressure to do more. I fall asleep in his arms, feeling cosy and safe.

**December 24th 2010**

A twinge of guilt disturbs my already fretful sleep. It's Christmas Eve and I always spend it with Mum and Dad and Abby. It was Abby's birthday a few days ago. I missed it. I didn't even remember until the day after. What kind of sister does that make me? Another reason to feel guilty. She's nine now, unbelievable. I doubt she misses me though. She'll be all about the presents today. The tree will be up, beautifully decorated by Mum who likes to spend time carefully arranging the baubles. Abby will have put on a few of the paper angels and cotton wool Santa decorations that she's made but they'll get discreetly moved to the back so that it doesn't mess up the whole look.

The presents will be piled high underneath, each wrapped in different coloured paper for each person with perfect tags to match. The dinner plan will be written out and Dad will complain that Mum always does it the same way every year and then Mum will reply that if it works why change it? Abby will want to stay up and wait for Santa Claus but will be distracted by yet another bad Christmas movie.

This year is different, for me anyway. Michael's small tree in the corner of his lounge is like something out of a catalogue. No baubles, just silver tinsel symmetrically laid out around it. Five presents lay underneath it, wrapped in gold paper. This year I am living with my boyfriend. Do you know how exciting that is? I push thoughts of my family away as I gaze down at Michael.

He stirs next to me and smiles. We are sharing a bed now. It was totally my decision but I am ready now. I can't tell you how good it felt to cuddle up to a gorgeous older man in bed. When he touches the ever fading scars on my arms he whispers 'you don't need to hurt yourself anymore.'

We didn't do it, not yet. I'm not quite ready for that. I

can tell he wants to do it but he's so patient. He just strokes my naked body and tells me that he's ready whenever I am but always adds 'no rush.' I want our first time to be special. I'm not sure what that special looks like yet. Do I want rose petals scattered across the bed, candles lighting the room, soft music playing the background? Sasha would say I've been watching too many soppy films. Maybe I have, but it's more romantic than her doing it in the back seat of her dad's car. I don't want to tell Michael any of my ideas, I'm worried he'll think I'm a stupid teenager.

'I have an early Christmas present for you,' he whispers gently.

He has certainly given me a lot of presents recently, the advantages of having an older, rich boyfriend. He slides out of bed, looking at me mysteriously. Reaching into the wardrobe he produces a carefully wrapped pink tissue papered gift. He hands it to me. 'For you.'

I open it excitedly, my hands shaking. I tear at the lovely paper, reach inside and touch something silky. I pull out a pair of the most sexy knickers you have ever seen and a bra to match.

'They're so-,' I gasp. I have never seen anything like them, not even in Debenhams.

'Try them on.' I glance at him shyly. 'Go on. You'll look amazing.'

I take them into the bathroom, not wanting to spoil the surprise. I step into the bedroom again feeling naked. His face says it all: he's impressed.

'Wow. Just wow.' He is practically drooling. 'Come back to bed so I can see you properly.' I know this is the moment when we will do it. I also know I am not ready but I feel powerless to stop it. He has been so kind in buying me these. I can't throw them back in his face and say no. It will be good, I tell myself. He will be gentle I'm sure.

Nervously I climb back into bed. Instantly his hands

devour me as if he has waited too long. This is going too fast. I want him to slow down but he keeps going.

'Be gentle,' I whisper but I don't think he hears me above his groaning noises. It hurts. Why didn't anyone tell me it would hurt so much. It goes on and on, like it will never stop. I want to cry out but I don't want to seem like a little girl. Finally he goes limp and he slides out of me. I am so relieved. I thought it would be better than that. 'Sorry,' he says gently. 'It'll be less painful next time.' I nod trying to fight back the tears.

**December 25th 2010**

Christmas day and I wake up thinking about Mum. Guilty thoughts plague my mind and I can't shut them off. I should be at home with them. Will I ever see them again?

Every time I suggest going to visit them Michael says it is better this way. They would only try and persuade me to go back. He's right, but part of me wonders if I should introduce Michael to them. They would like him, I'm sure they would, but then the age gap makes me think they wouldn't. I mean he's only a few years older, but they wouldn't see it that way. I'm pretty sure Dad's older than Mum. How is this any different?

Dad would probably kill Michael if he'd known what had happened last night. I so wanted to enjoy it, savour my first experience of making love but no one ever told me it would be like that. It seemed so … well, mechanical. Surely it gets better?

Michael wakes up smiling at me.

'Merry Christmas,' he whispers. 'Come here.' He pulls me over to cuddle him. There's nothing like cuddling the man you love on Christmas Day.

We'd never talked about what we'd do at Christmas. I have no idea if he has family or if we'll see them. I could have said I'd like to see my parents but it's too soon. I'll leave it a few months when Mum isn't stressy.

'What's the plan for today?' I ask.

'The plan is I cook you a delicious Christmas Dinner and then we open our presents.' I already know that the presents I bought for Michael are going to be nothing in comparison to what he has bought me, cheap gifts compared to his exquisite and expensive ones. I only had a ten pound note that I'd nicked out of Mum's wallet before I left.

'You didn't want to see your family?' I ask tentatively.

'No way.' His face darkens a little, clearly it is too painful to talk about. 'We don't get on.'

'Oh right.'

'You don't mind that it's just the two of us do you?'

'Mind? No, of course not. I love spending time with you.' Which is true, I do, but it would have been nice to get out for a change to see someone else. I love him but being in one place together - I guess you need a break occasionally.

I think too much. It'll be lovely I'm sure.

'Great, then I'll go get started on our delicious lunch.' He reaches for his clothes and then smiles. 'Oh, and a little present to get you started.' He hands me a small gift wrapped in shiny red paper. I take it, beaming back at him. I squidge it like you always do with presents. It's soft, an item of clothing maybe? I slowly unwrap it to reveal a light pink scarf, not the winter kind but the one posh people wear with their beautiful tops.

'I love it,' I say putting it on despite the fact that I'm only wearing a thin night dress. I start to get up but Michael shakes his head.

'No, you stay here. You deserve your beauty sleep.' Of course there's no way I can get back to sleep now but I lay my head back on the pillow, smiling to myself. How lucky am I to be having Christmas lunch cooked by the man of my dreams. Mum's face forces its way back into my mind. I can't text her now even if I wanted to. Her Christmas lunches are usually the best: crispy roast potatoes, giant

Yorkshire puddings; she'll be getting it ready now, without me. The thought makes me sad. Abby will be rushing down to open her presents, eyes full of joy, not stopping until every last present is opened, wrapping paper strewn across every corner of the lounge. I don't need that childish stuff anymore. Maybe next year when it's all calmed down we can see them at Christmas. Mum will understand better then.

I hear voices from the lounge, the TV? It sounds like another man is in there. I didn't think anyone else was coming. I pull on my clothes, casual ones for now. I can always change for lunch. When I get in there Michael is cooking alone, humming to himself.

'Was someone here?' I ask.

He shakes his head. 'No. Only me.'

'I thought I heard something.'

'Must have been the radio.'

I glance at the radio which is still switched off at the plug on the wall. Strange but why would he lie? Better to change the subject.

'Can I help?'

'Nope, got it all under control. Why don't you go and watch TV.'

I leave, reluctantly. I'd like to help, to be near Michael not stuck in the lounge on my own. Some kids' Christmas movie is on. I don't bother to find anything else.

At the dinner table I miss the hustle and bustle of my house. Uncle Pete would be there in full force with his cringy bad jokes. The little cousins would be getting food everywhere and demanding to pull their crackers right now this minute and I, being the eldest cousin, would be expected to take control of them. Mum, stressing about whether the turkey is cooked or not, would be exhausted by the time she sits down.

In comparison, this year is so serene and quiet that I almost dare not speak. Michael proudly places down dinner plates with carefully arranged meat, potatoes and vegetables - no helping ourselves from the middle of the table. Dinner is small, not piled high like I'm used to at Christmas. I smile sweetly.

'This is lovely,' I say, and it is. Really it is. Michael looks very happy, happy that he was able to do this for me.

'For you, anything. Only the finest food is good enough for such a princess.'

We eat in silence, too busy concentrating on our food. By now I would have had my conversation interrupted several times by one of the kids or Uncle Pete, probably more likely him. He doesn't know how to engage in civilised conversation. I shudder at the thought of Michael meeting Uncle Pete. They are worlds apart in life. Michael would completely look down on him.

I am expecting dessert, well it is Christmas, but none arrives and I don't like to ask.

'Present time,' he announces when the plates have been cleared away.

We move to the sofa where Michael, treating me as if I were royalty, insists I sit down while he carefully selects the immaculately wrapped gifts and hands them to me. The first is the loveliest bracelet and necklace set I have ever seen, gold, delicate, perfect and so much more expensive than I am used to.

'It's beautiful, thank you so much.' I let Michael put the necklace on.

The remaining presents are a mix of perfume and clothes, all adorable. At last I am able to give him my presents but I haven't spent nearly as much as him. He smiles politely at the shirt I bought him. He will never wear it. He takes the aftershave and puts it on the side. I don't even know if that's his taste.

And then it's over, too soon.

Michael takes the pieces of wrapping paper and carefully folds them before putting them into the kitchen. I am wondering what will happen next, when his phone rings. He stabs the button aggressively.

'Not a great time.' He steps towards the bedroom glancing over at me apologetically. 'What really? … right …' Turning to me, he whispers, 'sorry I have to deal with a work related matter,' and shuts himself in the bedroom.

I am left alone wondering whether to watch another Christmas film.

When he returns fifteen minutes later I daren't ask what the call was about. He slides in next to me and complains about the choice of film until I hand him the remote.

I guess that was Christmas.

## January 15th 2010

Life goes on and I am still here with Michael. I think about my family all the time and wonder if I made the right decision leaving. I could go back but I feel silly. Also I do love Michael. He is so good to me. He was right, it wasn't as painful the second time and now it is almost good. I am so loved.

My only wish is that I could have avoided hurting Mum and Dad. I wonder if they are still looking for me. I wish I had a working phone so I could text them but Michael's right. It's better to make a clean break.

Today is like any other day: I clean the apartment, I watch TV, and then Michael arrives home seemingly distressed, almost crying.

'What's wrong?'

'Oh babe, I've been so stupid.'

'What have you done?'

'I got involved with some bad people.'

'What kind of bad people?' He sighs and turns away.

'It's okay, you can tell me.'

'I owe people money for drugs.'

'Drugs?' His eyes look down in shame.

'I'm sorry, I've let you down. I only have them sometimes. I'm not addicted. Only when I'm feeling low.

A pick me up, you know.'

'Yeah, course.' I don't know but I can't say that.

'Now they're after me.'

'Oh Michael. What are you going to do? I wish I could help.'

'I don't know what anyone can do.'

'There must be something that will keep them away.'

He pauses and smiles slightly. 'Well actually, maybe you can help.'

'I can?'

'One of them is Stuart, you know the one we went to dinner with in Marchello's?'

'Oh yeah, I remember him.' He was the more confident of the two men, bold and handsome.

'He wants to go on a date,' he says, turning to me, 'with you.'

I'm not sure whether to be flattered or surprised. The thought of another older man wanting to go on a date with me makes me feel good but surely he knows I'm with Michael.

'A date, nothing else.'

'So, like to dinner?'

'Yeah, Marchello's or something similar. He'll book somewhere and you go along, looking amazing as you always do, and he'll cancel the debt.'

'The whole debt?'

'So what do you think?'

'Well yeah, I guess so.'

'Thanks babe, you are amazing.' He runs over and kisses me hard on the lips. 'I promise I won't ask you to do it again.'

I nod. He disappears into the bedroom with his phone, presumably to make arrangements with Stuart. I sit down on the sofa, a bit unsettled. It'll be fine, just a dinner date. No big deal.

## January 17th 2010

The date is arranged for two days after. The night comes round quickly. I've met Stuart yet I feel nervous. Michael seems to sense my unease.

'It'll be fine.' I smile. What can I say?

Michael smiles as I stand before him for an inspection, dressed in my newest blue dress and jewellery. I feel stunning, like a princess. He nods and whistles. 'Gorgeous. Totally gorgeous.'

Stuart picks me up in his swanky car, a BMW. My friends would not recognise me right now. He looks me up and down approvingly as he holds the passenger door open and I climb into the front seat. I am instantly overwhelmed by the smell of his aftershave.

'Michael has good taste.' I smile nervously 'It's okay,' he says reaching over to hold my hand. 'This will be fun and painless.' I don't like the way he says painless. I suddenly long for the familiarity of Michael's apartment but it's too late now we are on our way.

It's only a dinner I tell myself. What could possibly be scary about a dinner?

The chosen restaurant is equally as posh as Marchello's. It's not one I've heard of but then I'm fifteen. My idea of posh is the Harvester. We are shown to our table.

'Your usual table, Mr Jones.'

'Thank you, Dean.' I sit down in the chair pulled out by Stuart. He sits himself down opposite me.

'So, Beth,' he pauses as I wonder if he is expecting me to fill the gap. 'Such a beautiful name.' I smile nervously and glance around at the smartly dressed couples around us. They seem so at home here, not like me. I'm so out of place. I'm half expecting at any moment that someone is going to call me out for being a fraud. *You don't belong here,* they'll shout. Stuart is still regarding me intently, maybe expecting me to say something intellectual. I only smile stupidly.

'You like the restaurant?' His accent is posh with a hint of Essex.

'Yes it's lovely.'

'Up to your usual standard I presume?'

I laugh. What does he think? That I always dine at places like this?

I order a chicken salad on Michael's instructions when I all want is burger and chips, not that they would do such a thing here. I eat slowly and politely, remembering my manners. Occasionally I stop and smile at Stuart. He raises his glass to me confidently.

'What a privilege to be at such a lovely restaurant with such a beautiful lady.'

A flash of his credit card at the waiter and he is bringing over the bill. A small blonde girl stares out of his wallet from a photograph - his daughter maybe? I wonder what kind of parent he is.

I am relieved when he is paying the bill and it is over. It was more than awkward, for me at least. I am tired. I just want to go back home, to Michael's apartment and go to sleep. I climb sleepily into the car next to Stuart.

'Don't look so tired. The night is young still.' I lay my head back confused at his words. 'Want to have more fun?' I sit up. I want to say no but I can picture Michael's face earlier, tear stained and upset. He leans over and puts his hand on my leg. 'The night is not over yet.'

He continues to drive past the point when I think we should be back.

'Where are we going?'

'Just back to mine for a night cap.'

I feel as though I'm being strangled. I want to shout at him to turn around, I want to jump out of the car but I don't. I am paralysed by fear and Michael's reaction. I don't want to let him down.

Stuart ushers me into his home. For a moment I forget the situation and stare gobsmacked at his massive house. High ceilings with stone flowers in every corner, exotic fish swimming gracefully around their bowl in the corner. I shiver with cold or fear, I'm not sure. I hesitate at the door.

'Don't be shy,' he sneers. There is no turning back now.

**January 18th 2010**

'He raped you?' Michael seems genuinely shocked.

'Yes,' I cry through tears that seem never ending.

'I'm so sorry babe. I had no idea he wanted that.'

'I didn't feel I could say no.'

He shakes his head angrily. 'Wait till I get my hands on him.'

'No Michael, you can't. Just leave it. It's done. Surely he'll leave us alone now.' Michael doesn't look so certain.

'Honestly I had no idea.' I believe him, why wouldn't I? I lay his head on my lap and comfort him.

'It's okay,' I say. Something feels wrong. Shouldn't he be comforting me? He lifts up his head and smiles gently at me.

'You are something special, you know that?' I smile shyly back and shrug. 'You are. You're amazing.' I soak up the compliments. He makes me feel special. Back home I was an average teenager, average looking, probably would have ended up with an average job. Now? Well now I have a smart older man to take care of me.

'I'm going to take you out tonight as a thank you. Where do you want to go? Your choice.'

I want to say Dominoes Pizza, on the sofa, staring at the TV, while trying not to cry. I rack my brains to think of somewhere that makes me sound a little bit sophisticated at least.

'Ask?' I suggest uneasily. He seems unsure but hides his look quickly.

'Sounds fabulous. I'll book us a table.'

He strides off, his previous worries now gone. I jump

into the shower, I need to rid myself of every trace of Stuart. I feel dirty. Visions of the small heart tattoo on his arm and the cold feel of that gold bangle against my back plague my mind. I hope the pill worked. At least what I have with Michael is real. Afterwards I lie on the sofa, torn between wanting to cry and sleep.

I must have drifted off as it's beginning to get dark outside. The orange glow of the sun setting is seeping through the edges of the curtains. I get up slowly, rub my eyes and sort out my hair. Then I wander over to the bedroom I can hear Michael's voice, presumably on the phone.

'I don't know Stu. You gotta give me more time … I know, I know but these things don't happen instantly … I get it … okay I'll see what I can do … yes, yes, just as gorgeous of course.'

I am puzzled. What is he talking to Stuart about? Shouldn't he be angry at him for the way he treated me? And what is going to take time? I ponder for a minute: what am I doing here? It is as if the sensible side of me has suddenly taken over and is asking what the hell is going on. It's fine, I tell myself. Nothing bad is going to happen. He loves me. Live a little. I am still wondering if I should go in the bedroom when he is at the door.

'How long have you been standing there?' Part of me wants to say 'long enough.' but I push that part away.

'Just got here,' I answer. I'm not sure he believes me. He smiles confidently and pulls me to him in a hug.

'I love you, you know that.' I murmur something that sounds like I know. I breathe in his manly scent, a mixture of expensive aftershave and clean clothes. 'Are you getting changed before we go to Ask?' It isn't really a question. I know it is what is expected of me. He would hate me going out to dinner in casual clothes. I'm not sure my posh dresses are suitable for Ask though, they seem a bit over the top. Then I remember the short dress I have, the only one I packed when I left home. That'll be perfect.

Michael smiles approvingly at it when I put it on.

'You'll do.' I can tell he's not as keen on the dress as me and I feel bad for disappointing him.

~

The restaurant is busy but I'm glad we're so far away from home. At least I won't meet anyone I know. I scan the room for familiar faces and stop when I see Sasha and her parents sitting in the corner. What is she doing here?

'Can we sit over there?' I point to the opposite end of the restaurant, out of sight of Sasha. While of course I would love to show off Michael I can't let her see me, what if she phoned Mum and Dad?

'Are you okay?' Michael seems to notice that I am jittery.

'Fine. Just hungry.'

'Me too,' he laughs.

We sit tucked away and I stare at the menu, holding it over my face. I choose pasta when I actually want pizza but I don't want him thinking that I'll put on weight. Pizza is so fattening. He's right. I don't need it.

'They don't have much choice here,' Michael comments. I want to point out that it has far more choice than some of his restaurants. But of course I don't. I ignore him and study the menu for the least fattening pasta dish.

'How about the fish?'

'I think I'm going to have the cannelloni.'

He raises an eyebrow. 'If that's what you want.' It's clearly not what he wants. 'It's your treat.'

We are halfway through the starter when I realise we are sitting on the route to the toilets. What if Sasha needs the toilet?

'You look anxious.'

'I'm fine. Just thinking.'

'Nothing too serious I hope.'

'No of course not. I was wondering how my parents are. Maybe I should call them.'

'I don't think that's a good idea.'

'Why not?'

'They'll only try and persuade you to come home.'

'Yeah, I guess.'

'Do you want to go back?'

'No, of course not. I love living with you.'

'Then forget about them and kiss me.' He pulls me over the table to him and kisses me, making me forget all about my parents and home. Why would I want to give this up? Out of the corner of my eye I spot Sasha walking by. I turn away but not before she sees me, her eyes widen. Damn it.

I have to talk to her. I make my excuses and follow her into the toilets.

'What are you doing here Beth?' she says in loud whispers. I could ask her the same question.

'I'm with Michael.'

'Who's Michael?'

'My boyfriend, you remember?'

'That old guy is your boyfriend!'

'He's not old. He's only 24.'

She looks doubtful. 'Of course he is.'

'He is. He told me.'

'Oh he told you then he must be.'

'You're jealous.'

'Oh give it up, Beth. Of course I'm not jealous. Can't you see what's happening?'

'Nothing is happening. I'm living with my boyfriend.'

'He's taking advantage of you. Have you slept with him yet?'

'That's none of your business.'

'You are fifteen. It's against the law. He could get arrested.'

'So what are you going to do? Tell on him?'

'I should. Your Mum has been going mad about you running away.'

'Sasha you can't tell. Please don't. He loves me.'

'Do you really think he would be interested in a fifteen year old?'

'Why wouldn't he?'

'You're so naive.'

I turn away. I don't need to listen to this anymore.

'Your Mum and Dad are distraught. Your Mum keeps phoning my house to check that I don't know anything. I swear she thinks I'm lying. She never has liked me. But you know what? A pain as she is, she loves you and I can see it's killing her, you being gone.'

'Stop,' I say. It's too much. 'Please, promise you won't tell.'

She goes into the toilet cubicle. 'I won't but promise me you'll think about it before you throw away your life with this nonce.'

I turn and leave the toilet. I don't need this. I don't need her guilt. I clonk heavily back to the table. I feel angry yet upset at the same time.

'What's wrong?' Michael asks.

'Nothing.'

'No, it's not nothing. Did you see someone in the bathroom?'

'Just an old friend.'

'An old friend?' He bounces his leg under the table.

'Don't worry. She's not going to tell anyone about us.'

'Do you want me to talk to her?'

'Please, just leave it. She's immature.' At that moment Sasha walks out, glaring at both of us. 'She doesn't understand.'

'Probably jealous,' he says smiling. I nod smiling back.

**January 19th 2010**

I didn't sleep last night, worrying that Sasha will tell Mum and Dad she saw me. What if she tells them and they try to find me? But she might not tell them. Who am I kidding? This is Sasha we're talking about, the girl who will blab your secret the first chance she gets.

*'Do I have to go to those interview rooms like in TV shows?'* She'd say. *'I'll only answer questions if a sexy policeman asks me.'* I chuckle at this. Mum will bug her constantly like she does with me. She won't leave her alone until she tells her everything which fortunately isn't much. She might tell them I was with an older man, no she'll definitely tell them that. Dad will be mad. I wonder if he'll act hard and threaten to beat them up for stealing his precious daughter but he has never cared who I hang out with before.

I'd be surprised if he could actually remember Sasha's name.

I weigh up the possibilities in my head. So she tells them, then what? Maybe they try and find me, question the waitresses at Ask? But what could they tell them? Only that I was there with a man. They won't know where I live unless Michael gave them his address when he booked. He's too clever to do that. I can't very well ask him. I can't question his judgement.

Sasha thinks she knows everything but she has no idea. I bet she's still a virgin. How could she even suggest that Michael is taking advantage of me.

He loves me, he does.

'What's up with you today?' Michael asks. I'm worried I have upset him.

'I'm fine, why?'

'You haven't sat down all morning. You've been pacing this living room like something's on fire.'

I sigh. I can't tell him but maybe I should. 'That friend last night. She'll probably tell Mum and Dad where I was.'

'And?' His angry tone scaring me suddenly. 'Why should that matter?'

'I don't want them knowing where I am.'

'And why should they? You are so naïve, Beth. How on earth will they know where I live?'

I shrug. I don't like his tone. 'I'm just scared.'

'Scared of what? Them?'

'I don't know. I don't want to ruin this.'

His expression softens. 'Oh baby, nothing is going to ruin this for us. You're a big girl now. Even if they found you they can't make you go home.'

'You think?' I'm not so sure.

'Of course not. You're old enough to live by yourself.'

'I guess so.'

'I know so. Now stop worrying about that girl. She's not worth the energy.'

~

My new phone arrives, it was delayed apparently, according to Michael. I immediately feel like texting Sasha to find out what she's said but I restrain myself. No point in making the situation worse. I'm not even sure I can remember her number. All those numbers were on my old phone. Very frustrating. A phone without any numbers in it feels quite sad and redundant. What am I supposed to do with it? I can log on to Facebook though.

'What are you doing?' Michael appears behind me, teacher like in his manner. Guiltily I try to hide it. I don't know why.

'Just having a go on my new phone.' He takes it from me.

'Facebook?' He asks, making me feel like a year seven. 'You don't need that. No one goes on Facebook anymore.' I want to tell him that my friends do but I don't argue with him. 'Don't waste your time on there. Come on we're going out.'

'Where?'

'It's a surprise.'

I forget Facebook and excitedly get my coat on and follow him out of the door.

The surprise trip is a drive in the countryside to Sudbury and the most beautiful riverside walk.

'I love this place.' He sighs longingly. 'Used to spend my childhood holidays here.' His smile lights up his face, it makes me love him even more. 'Before- '

'Before what?'

He seems like he wants to tell me something. 'Nothing. It's not important.' I want to tell him it is important because I care about him but his face has a closed expression now and I don't want to push it. 'Look over there.' He directs my eyes to a flock of birds, the largest I have ever seen.

'What are they? They look like storks.' He laughs.

'They're herons.'

'Amazing.' We stand there watching as a couple paddle by in their canoes, swiping furiously from side to side with such determination. It would be great to do that, to glide along the river without a care in the world.

'We used to do that too,' Michael says pointing at the canoes.

'Was it fun?'

'Great fun.'

'Who's we?'

'My brother and I.'

'I didn't know you had a brother. Are you close?'

'We were until- ' His expression darkens. 'It doesn't matter. Let's just say we fell out over a few things.'

'Every sibling has fights. My little sister and I fight all the time though she always wins because she's so much younger and runs to Mum.' I instantly regret saying that, reminding him that I'm only a teenager. His face doesn't change as he takes my hand.

'My parents were strict. I never felt good enough.'

'I know that feeling going to a grammar school. They expected perfection.' He squeezes my hand tightly.

'Do you know what? You're something special.' A surge of happiness flows through me as he gazes intently at me. 'This is so relaxing here, by the river, with you. I wish it could always be like this.'

## March 2010

I like the view from Michael's apartment. You can just see the little flowers shooting out of the cold hard ground, colourful buds with tiny green leaves. Spring is on its way, the warmth of it streaming in and lifting my spirits. I remember the way that Abby used to point out the flowers in our garden. She loved them, especially the roses. The birds are happy too, chirping noisily outside the window.

I am legal now. I was sixteen two weeks ago. The thought scares me, I don't know why. Michael took me out, just the two of us. It should have been special but I missed my family; I wondered if Mum and Dad even remembered that it was my big birthday. Sweet sixteen, yet not so sweet anymore.

My life was innocent back then. Things have changed and I don't know what to do. Michael got in trouble again, this time with a different man, Steven, so I had to go on another "date". He promised me it would be the last time but I'm starting to question what to believe anymore. I love him and I know he loves me but I am spiraling into something I can't control.

We have these special moments where he is so attentive to me then at other times he is cold and I don't know who he is.

Steven was a lot gentler and it wasn't an altogether a horrible experience. I kept reminding myself that I was helping Michael. He cried when he asked me: told me that they would kill him if he didn't send me on this date. What could I do? I want to leave but Michael said if I ever left they'd come and find me and kill me too. He said it in such a gentle tone that the words almost didn't match his expression. I don't know what to think anymore.

Now it seems my life is full of "dates". Sasha would say I'm a prostitute but it's not like that. I'm doing Michael a favour. If it keeps them off his back then it's worth it.

I almost phoned Mum yesterday. Michael had gone out

and I picked up the phone. I dialled her number but then something stopped me. I couldn't complete the call.

I consider trying again today. I punch in the numbers, I will myself to have the courage. Michael appears suddenly behind me.

'What are you doing?'

I throw down my phone in shock but it falls onto the sofa with the screen facing upwards showing my little secret for all the world to see.

'You silly girl. Don't do it. If you phone home they'll hurt your family too. Is that what you want?'

'No, of course not.' Tears begin to flow down my face. 'I just want to talk to Mum.'

'I know, I know you do sweetheart but it's too dangerous. I promise it won't be this way forever. We'll go away, just you and me, away from the nasty bad men. Then you can call them when we get there.' I nod as I pick up my phone and cancel the number.

'That's a good girl.'

I am so confused. I want to leave, to go home. But I love being with Michael in this apartment.

I don't want to go on any more "dates".

That evening we dine in Michael's favourite posh restaurant. I've almost forgotten what burger and chips look like, it's been so long. I kind of like salad now. It makes me feel sophisticated. If Sasha could see me here, she would be so jealous. The intimate dinner I thought it would be turns into a dinner with his friends. Stuart, Steven and two new men I haven't met before, Henry and Joe. I wonder if those are their real names. Something in me doubts it.

They smile at me while ignoring me at the same time. I am special yet forgotten.

I long for the fun meals with my friends where we could laugh and stuff chips into our mouths, where we were out to impress no one. Where did it all go wrong? My stomach muscles tense up as Henry and Joe stare at me somewhat leeringly. I know what they want now. My hands shake as I try to pick up my fork. I can't do this. I need to get out. Michael seems to sense something is not right. He throws me a loving look and puts his hand on my arm. It works. I feel calmer already.

The meal seems to last forever. I barely eat. I want to get out of there.

Finally we go home alone. I am relieved. Michael takes me lovingly to bed. I should tell him there and then that these "dates" must stop but how can I? As he lies half-awake next to me I summon the courage.

'I can't do it anymore.'

'What can't you do?'

'All the "dates".'

'Oh Beth. I know, I know. I promise it won't be long.'

'That's what you keep saying. And it won't stop with Stuart and Steven will it?' Michael turns away and I know I have hit close to the truth. Then suddenly his expression changes.

'Look Beth, you wanted this.'

'Wanted what?'

'The whole exciting life away from your parents.'

'Yes I did but it didn't involve being a prostitute.'

'Oh seriously, Beth, did you think life was all cotton candy?'

Suddenly I am seeing a side to Michael I don't like. I get out of bed.

'Where are you going?'

'I'm going home.'

'Wait no, Beth I'm sorry.'

'It's too late.' I pull my clothes on furiously. As much as I do not want to go home, back to my ordinary life, I can't do this anymore. Michael jumps out of bed naked and grabs hold of my arm.

'You're not going anywhere.' I try to wrench myself free but he merely holds on tighter. 'You can't just walk away from this.'

'I am,' I scream, trying desperately to escape. Breathing heavily, he throws me on the bed. I shrink back into the corner of the bed and hug myself.

'You are not going anywhere,' he repeats firmly. He pulls on his underpants and reaches into his chest of drawers. Unable to move I watch as he pulls out a key which he locks the bedroom door with from the inside. 'As I said, you are *not* going anywhere.'

Fear sweeps through me, flooding my insides, as I wonder what he is capable of. How stupid could I have been? I need to get out of here. As he falls asleep next to me at least, I console myself; he can't make me do any of those nasty things anymore; he can't make me go on dinners I don't want to go on; and he can't force me into a car, because if he does I will run and keep on running.

I don't sleep for hours. My mind is racing as I consider the different ways I can escape. I am stupid. Everyone will think I am a silly girl. Only silly girls fall for such tricks. Michael starts snoring and I glance over at my pillow. I could suffocate him and go. At least then I would be free. I know I will never be able to do it but the thought that I could comforts me.

The next morning he wakes up and smiles at me, as though our conversation last night never happened.

'I'm sorry if we had a little fight.' His gentleness touches me and I see the old Michael returning. He kisses me and I can feel myself softening towards him. 'I would be heartbroken if you left me.' He strokes my face with such care that I find it hard to believe that it was ever any different. 'I won't hurt you. I promise. Please forgive me.'

What choice do I have? Ultimately I love him. I am invested in him and our relationship.

'I promise I won't make you go on any more dates.'

I smile.

'Okay,' I whisper and I let him have me again. My heart soars and all the feelings of hopelessness dissipate.

I love him, I can't deny that.

**April 2010**

No dates for weeks now. I am so happy with Michael. He hasn't locked the bedroom door again and life is all about us. We still go to restaurants but there has been no mention of Stuart or the others. Memories of my family are fading and I wonder why I wanted to go back. I feel so relaxed; life is so good. No worries, no stress, just the two of us.

Tonight Michael is late home. The apartment is unusually quiet. I miss him even though it has only been a few hours. When I finally hear the key in the door I realise he is not alone. I wait to see who will appear in the lounge but I know that voice. Fear takes over and I edge away from the sofa towards the bedroom.

'Hey, where you going?' It is Stuart. His greedy smile tells me all I need to know about why he is there. He pulls down the jacket of his expensive suit and runs his fingers through his hair. I seek help in Michael but he shrugs. I want to shout at him that he promised.

'Just tonight,' Michael says calmly. I don't have to ask him to explain further to know what he means. I hesitate. I should run but Michael has locked the door. I should say no, but with two men in front of me what chance do I have? Michael sidles up to me. 'Just tonight,' he whispers.

'No,' I hiss furiously. 'I don't want to.'

'You know why this is important.' He holds my arm in a tight grip. Stuart stands behind him, a smug look on his face. I know when I am defeated.

Michael hands me a drink that he has been holding and I find myself giving into his demands.

'Just tonight,' I whisper as I sip from the drink. Instantly the room starts to spin and my body doesn't feel my own. I attempt to walk but my legs won't work. Sleep starts to overtake me. What did he put in the drink?

I wake up in bed with Michael. I have no idea if anything happened with Stuart or even if he is still here.

'Thank you,' whispers Michael at me as he opens his eyes. I have no doubt what he is thanking me for and the wet feeling between my legs leaves me with no doubts as to what went on.

I should feel betrayed by the man I love but instead I am relieved. It is over and the best part is: I don't remember it. I want to believe that there will be no more nights but part of me doesn't. I let Michael cuddle away my worries as I drift off into unnatural sleep again.

*'Get back here Beth.' Angry men run after me. They keep shouting. I've got to get away but my legs won't work. I can't move, they are almost upon me. I have to get out of here. They are right behind me. The tallest man reaches for me.*

I sit up in bed, sweating, breathing fast.

Michael has gone from the space next to me. I hear the shower going. I lay my head deeper into the pillow to try and block out the dream and my life. I have to get out but I love him. I can't leave him but how can I stay with him? A million thoughts swirl round and round in my head until I wish I could escape them. I close my eyes in an effort to get back to sleep but they won't stop. The thoughts keep on and on, threatening to explode in my mind.

'Hey babe.' Michael stands before me with only a small towel to cover him. I try to smile but worry that he will see through my inauthentic expression. 'You okay?'

How can I tell him I am not?

'Fine. A bit groggy.'

'I thought we could go for a romantic walk in the forest, far from here.'

'Sounds lovely.' And it does. Getting out of here is what I need right now. He dries himself off in front of me, smiling as I admire his body, the way his muscles form so perfectly and how the dragon tattoo fits so nicely around them.

To see us walking in the forest, hand in hand laughing, you'd think we were any other couple. The fresh air makes me feel alive again. The cool breeze gently rushes past me.

I see the admiring looks that Michael gets as we pass other couples. I am proud he is my boyfriend. He's everything I could want in a man except … no, I don't want to think about that. I can't think about that. Michael is my boyfriend and that is all there is to it.

We sit for a while by the lake and watch the ducks. I admire their freedom. They can fly away whenever they want to. A moment of sadness threatens to engulf me as Mum and Dad and Abby come into my mind. I wonder how they are. They've probably forgotten about me by now, moved on. Abby certainly will have. I suddenly long for them but Michael's hand squeezing mine brings me back to reality, he seems to sense my thoughts. Why do I have to sacrifice them for him? Why can't I have both?

'Come on, let's go.' He stands up and pulls me to my feet. 'It'll be time for lunch soon.' I allow myself to be led by him and wonder when it will end. I know it wasn't only last night. There will be another night, another Stuart. Right now seeing Michael's tender smile I can't imagine there will be but in my heart I know. We walk slowly through the woods to the main road where it's a short walk back to his apartment.

**May 2010**

Michael arrives at the door with a girl. 'Beth, this is Isabella.'

I'm guessing she's younger than me. She has pretty, beautiful blonde hair. Easy to see why anyone would fall for her. She is instantly a threat to me. Fear is written all over her face.

'Can you look after her today?' He doesn't give any more explanation. When I try to push him for more he shrugs me off. 'I have to go,' he says urgently.

I have no idea who Isabella is or what she is doing here. I don't like it and I don't like having to babysit her. She sits down on the sofa awkwardly. She should be at home; she's far too young to be out on her own.

'What are you doing here?' I ask her finally, fed up of trying to ignore her.

'I'm supposed to be at school,'

'Why aren't you then?'

'Because Michael said he'd look after me. I can't go home.'

'What do you mean you can't go home?'

'My dad … he'll hit me.'

'Hit you. Why?'

'That's what he does. Well, he's my step dad. Mum loves him and I thought he'd make her happy. I had to get away. Then I met Michael.'

I am torn between wanting to help this poor girl who is being thrown from one bad situation to another without even realising it and tearing her eyes out with jealousy, for even daring to come near my Michael. Obviously I can't do the second one. I am not sure how I can help though either. He's my Michael, how can I make her understand that?

'Be careful,' I grunt.

'What do you mean?' Her innocent eyes widen with terror.

How to explain months of explicit moments where I have been divided between different men, but felt loved and used at the same time.

'He's not who you think he is.'

'What do you mean?'

Should I warn her of what's to come? If she ran away now would Michael be angry?

'He has a temper,' I say finally. I can't tell her the whole truth.

'Like my step dad?' She looks terrified, like a bird ready to take flight.

'No, not that. He doesn't hit, he gets angry sometimes. Be careful, that's all.'

'Okay, thanks.' I feel that all I have achieved is to confuse her.

~

Before I know it Isabella has become my new roommate. We even sleep in the same bed. If it was strange to start with after a while it becomes normal like it was always meant to be. Michael is often out at night and Isabella and I become good friends. I start to enjoy life again with someone to keep me company. It's good to have someone to share thoughts with. We laugh, we do silly things and I begin to hope that this is how it will always be but as with all good things I know it must come to an end.

It ends abruptly one night when Michael arrives home with Stuart. I don't know if he is here for me or Isabella, or even both.

'We're going out.' Michael looks at me. I am wearing my jeans and tee shirt. 'Get changed.'

I glance over at Isabella fearfully who has no idea what is about to happen. She seems excited and is even more so when she realises that Michael has bought her a posh dress too. She acts like I did when I first got to go out all dressed up. I consider warning her, telling her that it's not innocent, but I don't want to burst her bubble. Michael ushers me out before I can say a word to her.

He smiles at us both in the taxi. 'Don't you two look gorgeous.'

Isabella beams proudly but I am uneasy, she has no idea what he's letting her in for. We arrive at Rocher, one of the middle posh ones. Even in my expensive dress I feel under dressed compared to other guests.

Sensing my discomfort, Michael says, 'It's fine. You look lovely.' The waiter doesn't even bat an eyelid as he shows us to the table.

Michael tries to talk to me several times but I am distracted.

'She'll be fine,' he reassures me. All I can do is nod. I am afraid I will cry if I say anything. Shortly after dessert

Isabella disappears off on the arm of Stuart. She clings onto him like she is going on a trip to the zoo. I think she has had too much to drink. I want to reach out and save her but it's too late. What could I do even if I wanted to?

~

The Isabella we return home to is a shell of the girl we left. Stuart has already gone and Michael doesn't hang around. She won't even look at me as she lies in the bed facing the wall. I climb into bed next to her, I am the worst friend ever.

'Why didn't you tell me?' she asks finally, her voice shaky.

'I'm sorry,' are the only words I can manage. There is no excuse. I should have told her, warned her to run the minute I saw her.

'How do we get out of here?'

How do I tell her there is no getting out?

**May 2010**

The smoke alarm screams at us, deafening me and Isabella.

'Make it stop,' she yells.

I frantically waft a sofa cushion below it.

'Open a window,' I shout. Isabella does as she is told and in an instant the alarm stops and the smoke begins to drift out of the window.

'What the bloody hell were you doing in there?' Isabella looks down guiltily.

'I got distracted.'

'You almost burnt the place down.'

I know I am being unreasonably angry but something inside me has snapped, the tension and stress that has been threatening to send me over the edge has now broken free and I can't control it.

'You idiot. What do you think Michael would say if he came home to a burnt out apartment? You're so stupid.' I keep yelling until Isabella screams out in frustration.

'Stop! I'm sorry!'

The fear I see in her mirrors my own feelings and I crumble. The anger slips away and I fall onto the sofa, tears escaping from my eyes. I feel as though a knife has been stuck in me. I can't stop. I am shaking. I am crying. I feel like I'm having a breakdown. It's the end of the world. Isabella stares at me with the same look of terror. I cry until I am exhausted and can cry no more.

'I'm sorry,' I sob.

She looks calmer now. I feel her soft touch as her fingers run through my hair like she is stroking a cat. 'It's okay Beth,' she whispers even though we both know it isn't.

'I'm sorry.'

'Shush, it's fine.' She continues to stroke me until my eyes begin to droop and I can only hear her sweet voice. 'We'll get out, don't worry.'

~

When Michael returns we are both curled up at opposite ends of the sofa watching a mushy film. I couldn't even tell you what it was about. Michael sniffs the air loudly as he comes in.

'You burn something?' he snaps rudely.

'Toast,' answers Isabella quietly. Michael shakes his head.

'Can't leave you two alone for a minute.' As he walks towards the kitchen he adds, 'Get ready. We're going out.' Isabella and I look at each other. Going out is the last thing I want to do and I can tell she feels the same.

Sometimes it makes me angry that no one has come to rescue me, not even my parents. If they loved me that much they'd find me, I tell myself. At other times I am terrified. What if they don't want to find me? What if they are glad to be rid of me? What if I never get found and have to live here forever? I push away these thoughts as Isabella and I endure a dinner with Michael and his friends.

What I previously thought of as flattering I now find disgusting, the way they look at us, undressing us with their eyes. How could I have been so stupid to get myself into this? I deserve this. I'm a stupid naïve girl. No wonder Mum and Dad are glad to be rid of me. Maybe now they can start afresh with Abby, do a better job.

Isabella clutches my hand in the back of the car on the way back. I squeeze it back to reassure her. My look says that we will get through this. I have to be strong for her even if I don't feel it myself.

~

'I think I'm pregnant.' Isabella's voice whispers in the darkness as we lie in our bed.

I wonder if I am dreaming. I could have easily drifted off. 'Beth?'

I sit up and turn to her. 'How do you know?'

'I'm late by about a week. I'm normally like clockwork.'

'Shit.'

'What are we going to do?'

I want to scream that this is her problem not mine but I don't. It is my problem now whether I like it or not.

'Beth?'

'Wait, give me a minute to think.'

'Sorry.'

'Did Michael not give you the pill?'

'I think I forgot to take one.' I shake my head

'I don't know what we're going to do but I need to sleep. We can talk about it in the morning.'

'Okay.'

Of course I don't sleep, how can I? Despite feeling exhausted my mind won't switch off. It goes through all the options, none of which are favourable. Eventually it is three am and I am being driven mad.

'Isabella, are you still awake?' I know she is because she has been tossing and turning next to me, another reason I can't sleep.

'Yes.'

'We need to get out of here. It's the only way. Then you can make a decision about what to do with the baby. Otherwise it'll be their decision.'

'I don't know if I can get rid of it.'

'You don't need to decide that right now.' When did I get to be the mature one? I never thought at sixteen years old I'd be stuck in an older man's apartment mentoring a younger girl who is pregnant.

'How do we get away?'

'I don't know yet but I'll figure it out.'

~

Of course if it was that easy we would have done it already. Michael always locks the door. When we are out he keeps a very close eye on us but there has to be a way out of here. The next day I stare at the lock on the front door, could I pick it? What do I know about picking locks? I study the window and wonder if we could climb out of it. But what if she fell and lost the baby? What about the window in the bathroom in Marchello's? It's a ground floor restaurant and the window is large enough for us to climb out. Why didn't I think of that before? So I do the only thing I can which is bide our time until our next dinner at Marchello's.

Fortunately for us it's only two days away. Michael is unusually excited because there are extra guests coming, even more reason for us to escape. I tell Isabella the plan in whispered tones. I stress the importance of staying calm, her excitement will give the game away.

I find it difficult to eat and to not get excited myself. I try not to think about where we will go. I haven't thought that far ahead. I just know we have to get out. If I seem unusually twitchy, Michael doesn't notice. I am relieved. The last thing I need is him questioning me. The moment we've been waiting for finally arrives: we've eaten our starters.

'I need the toilet,' I mutter as I slide out of the seat. I don't even look at Isabella. I don't trust myself to. Any look could give the game away. I walk slowly to the toilets, I'm shaking. This has to work. I calmly go to the toilet and then wait by the sink. Isabella appears through the door right on time.

'Was he suspicious?' I ask.

'He was a bit grumpy but no. I told him we both had our girly time.'

'Right, you have to be careful when you are climbing out.' I don't want to keep going on about the baby but I don't want her to lose it. She nods and steps up onto the bin. Carefully she opens the window fully and climbs up onto the ledge. She glances back nervously at me.

'Go,' I say impatiently. She disappears out of the window and I climb up to follow her. I glance down through the window and she is standing at the bottom, grinning fearfully. I quickly ease my way out. We've done it.

I grab her hand and lead her out of the backyard, through the gate and onto the pavement. I have to think quickly. I have to get us out of here before they come looking. I pull her down the street away from the restaurant. I don't stop, I don't look back. We need to get out of there.

'Where are we going?' she asks anxiously. I don't reply because I don't have an answer.

We take a few right turns and left turns until we are completely off the track.

'Stop, I can't run anymore,' she puffs.

'Sorry. We'll stop here and figure it out.'

So this is freedom. Freedom from scary men who want things they shouldn't. Freedom, yet I feel so scared.

**June 2010**

The sky is beginning to get dark as the sun slowly retreats into the distance. We need to find somewhere to stay tonight. We can't sleep on the street. I consider going home, asking Mum and Dad to take me back but what if they said no? What if they said yes to me but not to Isabella? I don't want their rejection. Why should they take me back? I wish I could go back to the Michael I knew in the early days, the one who would do anything for me.

I am about to cry with frustration at our situation when I see a hippy looking woman standing on the street corner giving out pots of food to homeless people. Her colourful linen trousers with weird patterns and streaky pink hair in dreadlocks makes her stand out a mile. I nudge Isabella, she shrugs wearily.

'I'm so hungry,' I say. She nods.

The woman scrutinises us suspiciously. 'You lost ladies?' I realise we are still dressed in our finest dresses, hardly the look of someone homeless.

'We're in trouble,' I reply, hoping she is the right person to tell. Beyond the suspicious face I can see kindness.

'What kind of trouble?'

I glance around me to make sure Michael or any of the men aren't following us.

'We have men after us.'

'Men?'

I sigh not wanting to go into details but knowing I will have to. Then out of the corner of my eye I see Michael. I panic. I grab Isabella's hand and get ready to run but something about the way he looks at me freezes me to the spot. His eyes are kind, his expression is concerned. Isabella screams, clutching my hand tighter.

'Girls, I've been looking for you.'

The hippy girl gives him a hard stare, she is ready for a fight.

'Beth can we talk? In private.' I know I should say no but I feel myself giving in to him yet again. I nod, to Isabella and the hippy woman's horror. I pull free from Isabella's grip and let him guide me to the entrance of a shop. The shop is dark but I can make out the shadows on the mannequins staring out at me accusingly. Michael gently touches my arm.

'Darling, I know things have been difficult recently and I admit I've been very stressed. I've probably taken it out on you.' I don't deny it. 'But please don't leave me. You are the only good thing in my life. The men are after me and I don't know what to do.' I want to tell him to stick it and stand up to them himself but I know it doesn't work that way. 'I promise I will never hurt you if you come back. I will take care of you and Isabella. Let me show you my love again.'

I so badly want him. Even his arm touching mine sends jolts of electricity through me. 'I will come back if you don't make me see any of those other men again.'

He looks unsure but nods. 'I won't.'

'Or Isabella?'

'Fine. I just want to be with you again.' And I want to be with him too. I know it's crazy but I love him. I can't live without him. 'Can we go home now?' He smiles a little pleading smile.

'Yes,' I laugh at his boyish expression. I bounce back over to Isabella and the hippy woman.

'It's sorted now. Sorry to bother you.' Isabella looks horrified. I send her a look which is meant to silence her. She opens her mouth as if to protest but then shuts it again.

The pink haired woman is less convinced. 'You don't have to be afraid of him,' she spits out

'I'm not,' I say confidently. 'It's fine. You don't need to worry now.' I take Isabella's arm and guide her in Michael's direction. 'Come on let's go.'

'You don't have to do this,' she shouts.

'I know.' I'm annoyed now but we continue to walk without turning around.

~

When we get back, Michael can't do enough for us. He is attentive to every little need. He cooks us a lovely meal and puts on a film. Isabella seems wary and there is still the problem of her potential pregnancy. I know she is going to ask me what to do tonight but I don't know. I don't want all this hassle. I've decided I want a simple life.

To my surprise, Isabella goes to sleep without a word. I wonder if she is angry with me but I don't want to ask in case it brings other unwanted questions. I must have been tired after our little adventure as I sleep through right until nine am. When I wake up, Isabella is not next to me. My body is a heavy weight, I can barely move it. I stagger to the lounge. Michael is reading a book in the corner of the sofa. There is no sign of Isabella.

'Where's Isabella?'

'She's gone.'

'Gone where?'

'She went to live somewhere else.' I'm delighted to have Michael back to myself, to be a proper couple again, but I'm also panicking. Where has she gone? What if he's hurt her? What will she do about the baby? 'Don't look so worried. She's gone home.'

'Home? As in with her parents?'

'Yes, she couldn't bear to be without them. She's not as mature as you.' He stands up and strokes my face. 'From now on it's you and me babe.' I am relieved but guilt wracks through me for feeling this way.

'I love you,' he says and my heart melts.

'I love you too.'

~

We make slow, tender, passionate love. Afterwards he cooks me the most romantic breakfast, every piece made with love. How lucky am I? I have the most wonderful boyfriend. I forget about the other stuff, the other men, Isabella. It's just me and Michael together again.

## June 2010

'You know I would never hurt you.' Michael strokes my head as I lay on the bed next to him. I wish I knew that. I love him. I have to take the chance. I think of Isabella back at home, safe in her own bed. I wonder if she's taken a pregnancy test yet or if she's told her parents. I smile at Michael. I'm glad I'm with him.

I must have drifted off because when I wake up it is dark and I am alone. I can hear voices coming from the lounge, urgent, desperate voices.

'Leave her alone.' Michael's voice sounds pleading.

'We had a deal.' Stuart. I should have known it was him.

'I know, I know but I love her.' Stuart laughs a horrible evil mocking laugh.

'Love? You don't even know what love is. Listen Michael you have until tomorrow evening to do the right thing or the deal is off.'

The whole apartment shakes at the sound of the front door slamming. A glimmer of light seeps through a crack in the door as Michael slowly pushes it open. He sighs and sits on the end of the bed. I dare not breathe let alone move.

'Are you awake?' he whispers.

I consider staying silent but I can't. 'Yes'.

'We need to get out of here.'

'And go where?'

'Do you trust me?'

After everything that has happened I shouldn't, but I do.

'Yes.'

'Get some more rest. We have a long journey today.'

Of course I can't sleep anymore. I wonder where we are going. I'm scared. I don't know if I want to move further away. Running away is one thing but this seems a step too far.

As soon as I am up, Michael is hurrying me along. He seems anxious. I'm full of mixed emotions at the memories I've had in his apartment. It feels right though, to get out of here, a fresh start.

We travel for almost an hour before I see the sign that welcomes us to Suffolk. Endless fields surround us and roads narrow into country lanes. The sun is beginning to go down but you can still make out the features of the cottage as we arrive. It couldn't be any more different than his apartment. It has charm oozing out of the thatched roof. The pink exterior walls delight me. So romantic, it could be in a Jane Austen novel. There is barely another house in sight. The road is empty, the kind that doesn't have a street light and will be completely dark at night.

'Here we are,' Michael announces.

I am filled with hope. Together we can build a new life here away from those nasty men. He kisses me as he unlocks the front door. I feel as if I am stepping into my dream home, cosy and full of character.

'I'm sorry for everything.'

I smile in response and stroke his hair. He has already been forgiven.

The lounge even has a log fire in it, perfect. I imagine us cuddling up on the sofa. I flop happily down onto it with a massive grin on my face, it is so soft you could sink right into it and not ever get up.

Michael laughs at me. 'Make yourself comfortable.'

'Oh I will, don't worry.'

'Come on, I'll show you the rest of the house.' He drags me up by the hand and takes me to the kitchen, a typical cottage style arrangement. It even has one of those Aga type things. Not exactly sure what that is but Mum used to rave about them. Seems like something posh people have.

The view outside reveals a massive garden with a rope swing down the end. I almost wish Sasha were here. She'd love it and we could run around together.

'No burning that toast here,' he jokes, shaking his finger at me. I laugh but I wish he hadn't mentioned it. It reminds me of all the awful stuff that has happened before. I push it out of my mind. This is our new start. We are safe here.

Keep telling yourself that.

'And … tada …  a dishwasher.' He tugs at the door and flings it open excitedly. I give a nod of approval.

'Come on, let's christen the bedroom. I'll beat you upstairs.' Like a young couple in love, on holiday, we run up the stairs. This is so amazing. I could certainly get used to it here. The bed even has posts around it. What do they call it? Four poster, that's it. A fairy tale bed. Sasha really would be jealous now.

I have the best night's sleep. In the morning, a note sits on the pillow where Michael slept.

*Gone to get supplies.* I lay my head on the pillow and stare up at the patterned ceiling.

Eventually I drag myself up and put on my silk dressing gown, the one Michael bought for me. I stare at myself in the mirror. I have to admit I do look good.

When Michael returns he makes me a full English breakfast. This really is a holiday.

'I could get used to this,' he says smiling and flipping the bacon over. Proper food as well. None of that salad rubbish.

'It's delightful,' I reply, wondering if I have just stepped out of Pride and Prejudice. Michael raises an eyebrow in humour at my expression.

'Aw, I love you.'

'I love you, too.'

This is our new start.

I am safe.

**July 2010**

It isn't long before the cracks start to appear in my fragile dream. The long nights alone, Michael's mood swings, the strange phone calls; all of which make me suspicious that nothing has changed. His frequent trips to Ipswich on 'business' make me wonder. Then one day Michael comes home beyond happy, his face alive with excitement.

'We're going out for dinner.'

I am glad to get out of this tiny cottage that I had once thought so idyllic. What was at first cosy and romantic has become stifling and restrictive. I pull out one of my best dresses, hoping it hasn't got dust on it, it's been that long. As I slide it on I stare at myself in the mirror and am excited but fearful of what this dinner will entail.

I've never been to Ipswich before. Its busy and slightly seedy looking streets are a stark contrast from the countryside we have just left. The restaurant is, of course, up to Michael's usual standards, stylish and exclusive, next to the river, with boats and tall buildings surrounding it. I am relieved when we are shown to a table by ourselves. However my relief is short lived when two men, in suits, arrive, smarmy and leering as Stuart was. I shoot a look of fear at Michael as he beckons them over.

'Don't worry babe,' he says casually. But I am worried. I don't want this again. Suddenly I am finding it hard to breathe. My dress feels too tight, my palms are sweating.

'You must be the lovely Beth,' says the first man approaching. He shakes my hand firmly, I smile weakly, eager to get away. The other man gives my back a slight rub as he shakes my hand. I pull away rapidly and sit down. The men begin making small talk and I switch off, wondering how this night will end and how I will get away. Then something makes me tune in again.

'How's the house?' The second man asks Michael. He glances awkwardly at me but if he is hoping I haven't heard, it is too late.

'All good. The girls are getting on fine.' What house? What girls? 'They are bringing in lots of business.' I naively wonder what they are talking about until the full horror hits me like a bolt of lighting. Seeing my face, Michael throws them a look that makes them shut up. A whore house! Michael is running a brothel full of prostitutes! I had never thought it possible. I don't know what I am feeling: anger? Shock? I have to get away.

'Excuse me,' I say pushing past both men to get out. 'I have to go to the toilet.'

Concerned, Michael asks, 'Beth, you good?'

'Fine,' I say hurriedly.

'She'll be okay,' I hear him say to the others. Already I can hear him continuing on with the conversation, my feelings don't matter.

I don't go to the toilet but instead run out the door. Michael and the other men are too busy talking about their nasty schemes to notice. I berate myself for my continued stupidity. I ignore the waiter's confused expression as I run past him but I keep going. I have to get out. A sense of urgency makes me run as fast as I can, which is not easy when you are wearing a tight dress and high heels. Tears begin streaming down my face. I am stupid. I am so stupid. I take my shoes off and throw them angrily at a shop entrance.

'Beth,' Michael's voice calls from behind me. I stop and turn to face him. His eyes are a mixture of fear and anger. 'Please don't go.'

I clutch the side of the shop to steady myself before launching myself off it. I have to run. I propel myself round the corner. I don't dare slow down, just in case.

'Beth, come back now!'

He's still there, gaining on me, sounding angrier by the minute. I force my feet to plod on along the cold pavement, ignoring the bumps and stones that cut themselves into my feet. I have to get away. I shoot a quick glance behind me, he is closer than ever, but it is a mistake. I misjudge the pavement and find I am flying across it. I land with a bump. I am sore; I can't even decide where it hurts. I have to get up. I have to go. A hand grabs me.

'You're not going anywhere.'

I try to shake free but his grip is firm. 'Let me go. I'm not coming back with you.'

'Where are you going to go?' he demands mockingly. 'Dressed like a prostitute, bruises down your legs. You're a mess.' His words hurt me deeply but something inside me snaps and anger takes over.

I kick him where it hurts. Immediately my arm is released. I hurt all over but I run. I can still hear him groaning in pain.

'Get back here you bitch!' He stumbles towards me but he is slowed down. I keep running, helped by the fact that I haven't just been kicked in the balls. I don't stop running until I bump into a homeless woman standing by the side of an empty shop. She looks annoyed, ready for a fight. Michael is nowhere to be seen.

'Hey, watch it lady!' she shouts.

'Sorry.' Her face softens when she sees how upset I am.

'Hey, what's wrong?' I shrug. Where to start? 'You shouldn't be out here alone, it's not safe.'

'I have nowhere to go.'

'What, in a fine dress like that? I don't believe it.' She eyes me suspiciously.

I sit down exhausted, on the step outside the shop, and begin to tell her my story of woe. I don't know why but I feel I can trust her. She nods and tightens her fist in anger in the right places.

'Sounds like that man of yours is taking advantage of you.'

'But he loves me. I know he does.'

'He may say he does but he's a liar. They all are. Why don't you go home?'

How can I explain that going home is not an option? 'I

know the place for you.'

She takes me to a women's refuge centre where the kindness of strangers makes me cry even more. They give me soup and a warm blanket. They don't force me to talk. They just take care of me. I am so relieved but now I don't know what to do next.

**August 2010**

'My name's Lily.' A girl, not much older than me, bounces up, full of enthusiasm with a broad smile. She examines me carefully, staring at my posh dress.

'I'm Beth,' I answer cautiously.

'We're sharing a room,' she says happily. I smile slightly. Lily seems friendly enough and I guess sharing a room with her will be fun. I notice we have an en-suite bathroom in our room and wonder if everyone has this privilege. I'm relieved. I hate the thought of trying to find the toilet in the middle of the night. It's modern, not what I expected.

She watches as I sit on the bed.

'Where's your stuff?'

'I didn't get a chance to get it together. I had to run away quickly.'

'From home?'

'Not exactly. I don't want to talk about it right now.'

'Of course. Sorry didn't mean to pressure you. How about I show you round this place?'

'That would be great but I should get changed first.'

The kind lady who invited me in gave me a bag full of clothes. Thank goodness. I can't stay in this dress forever, besides I'm getting a bit cold. I find a jumper and a pair of jeans, a far cry from what I am used to wearing lately, but it's a relief to wear normal clothes again.

The women's refuge is full of smiling staff who seem to love what they do. They go a long way to make me feel wanted and safe. I need that right now. Crying babies and older children running around echo the hallways as we tour the building. 'Are there a lot of babies here?' I ask, pointing at the buggy park by the front door, I had failed to notice it when I first came in.

'Quite a few I guess. It's pretty noisy here but you soon get used to it and to be honest I don't even hear the screaming babies anymore,' she chuckles.

I suddenly feel very young; compared to the other women. They are probably thinking I'm a silly teenage girl who got herself into trouble.

A small girl, about five years old, strides up to me confidently. She reminds me of Abby. 'My name's Jessica.'

'Hi Jessica. I'm Beth.'

'Are you coming to live here too?'

'Yes. Is that okay with you?'

She nods happily. 'Would you like to see my dollies?'

'I think Beth is having a tour right now. Maybe she can see them later.' A woman, presumably her Mum, grabs Jessica from behind. Jessica stamps her foot.

'I'll come back. I promise,' I whisper as I follow Lily out the door.

'The little kids can bug you a bit but just tell them to go away and they'll soon get the message.'

'It's fine. I'm used to little kids. I have a younger sister.'

'What a pain.' I smile at her idea of a pain. Maybe my view of Abby has got somewhat rose tinted though. 'This is the laundry room.'

I almost exclaim LAUNDRY ROOM, we have to do our laundry? But I don't. I kind of thought one of the staff would do it. How do you even work such a machine? I don't say this, of course. I don't want to appear a spoiled brat.

It takes about half an hour to get round the whole building, taking into consideration interruptions by small children. Everyone is friendly and no one has looked down on me yet.

I think I'm going to like it here.

Later Lily and I are lying on our beds in the dark when I suddenly feel the urge to tell all.

'I went off with an older man. He seemed lovely at the time, gave me lots of presents.'

'Oh yeah, one of them. You have to be careful of those types.'

'I wish I'd had someone to tell me that months ago, though I'm not sure I would have listened.' She nods. 'Michael was special. I thought he loved me but then he got other men involved.' I can't see her face in the dark but nothing about her manner suggests she is surprised by this.

'Forget him. You're here now. You don't need him.' I get the feeling she's eager for me to move off the subject.

'Yeah, so true.' I wish I could forget but I miss him so much. I miss his cuddles in bed.

~

I soon settle into this new normal here at the women's refuge. It's familiar and almost boring but at least I'm not in danger. Lily is full of life, always bouncing around as though she can't be contained. She's cagey on why she is here. I try to drag it out of her, all I know is it's something to do with an abusive boyfriend. I get the feeling she's embarrassed about it but hey you only have to look at my life, she has no reason to feel bad.

There aren't many rules except a ten pm curfew which annoys the hell out of Lily.

'What if we want to go clubbing?' she complains to me. The idea of clubbing right now scares me; the thought of hot and sweaty men groping me fills me with dread, too close to what I went through. It's probably where Michael and his friends find their next victims, shopping centres and nightclubs, ready to pick up the next naïve girl. How could I have fallen for it? Did I really think an older man would want me for me? Lily's right, men are only after one thing and it's not a thing I ever want to give again.

After a few weeks at the women's refuge, Lily begins to

look distracted, staring longingly out of the window.

'What's up?' I ask.

'I know it's nice and all here but wouldn't you like to live out in the world again?'

'What do you mean?'

'I mean, I know a house we can live in.'

'Is it … safe?'

'Yeah, sure it is. It's not even in Ipswich. No one would find us there.' Seeing my expression, she adds, 'We could have more freedom and not have to follow these silly rules.'

'There is a reason for that.'

'Yeah but it's not living is it?'

'I guess you're right.'

'I know I'm right.'

'But we haven't got any money. How would we manage?'

She takes an envelope out from under her mattress. 'I have.' I don't ask her where she got it from.

So that night we pack our things and announce we're leaving. The manager tries to persuade us to stay, even tries to persuade me to go home. I get that they're right but I can't do it, not yet. '*Sorry Mum, I ran off with a man and you were right. You know best.*'

I'm seriously not going to degrade myself like that. Besides they might not even want me back.

So we leave. Me, my new backpack they bought for me, the second hand clothes they gave me, ready to take our chances in the world.

The house Lily takes us to is an hour's bus ride away in what looks like the dodgiest area of town. Mum would have had a fit if she knew where I was. Not a place for a grammar school girl like me. A blonde girl meets us at the door.

'Hey Lily. Who's your friend?' She eyes me suspiciously and I have a sudden feeling that I wasn't invited.

'This is Beth. She won't be any trouble.'

'She better not be,' replies the girl sternly, without even looking at me. Apparently I don't even get to speak.

'That's Geri,' hisses Lily dramatically.

The house is filled with numerous lingering aromas, incense, weed. 'Fred, Steve.' Geri points to two men in the lounge as we enter it. 'Lily, Beth.'

'Hi,' they mutter.

I wonder how many more people they have crammed into this small house. I smile but no one seems to notice. Lily, on the other hand, plonks herself down on the sofa like she's always lived there.

'So what's up guys?' They stare at her, half bemused, half suspicious.

'Not much,' replies one of them. I am still standing in the doorway awkwardly, bag on my back.

'Sit down.' Lily pats the seat next to her. I do but find I am perching on the edge, not feeling entirely comfortable in this strange house.

This is our new life.

## September 2010

We quickly settle into our latest abode. It's not as safe and cosy as the women's refuge but Lily is right: it's exciting and we are free. We can come and go as we please without a mother figure hassling us. Fred and Steve never seem to warm to us. Lily tries, she tries so hard; she practically flings herself at them, demanding their attention, needing them to notice her but at most she gets a glance or a nod. At least they acknowledge her, I'm non-existent. Most of the time we exist separately next to each other. Sometimes it bothers me but at other times I'm glad to be somewhere safe, away from Michael.

Geri is a different story. She wants to know everything: why I'm here, how I met Michael, what he did to me, how I got away, and what I'll do in the future. It's exhausting but I can't very well tell her where to go.

Michael. The thought of him fills me with dread, yet I miss him and I miss the way he showered me with love.

I have to move on, I know I do, but it's hard.

~

A continuous loud knocking at the front door one morning startles us. We stare at each other, eyes wide open. Geri peeps out of the window.

'Tall tanned man,' she describes. I can feel the colour draining from my face. How did he find us here?

'It's Michael, isn't it?' says Lily. I nod frantically. 'Go upstairs, hide. We'll deal with this.'

I don't have to be asked twice, I leg it up the stairs, trying not to fall up them. I run to our room and slide under the bed taking my duvet with me and covering myself in it. I stick my ear out so I can hear what's going on.

'Where is she?' He's shouting. He's inside!

'She's not here,' Lily is saying.

'I don't believe you. I saw her. Is she upstairs?' He's banging on something angrily. I've never heard him like this before.

'Mate, chill out.' Steve's voice as he tries to calm him down. 'You need to leave.'

'Leave? Not until I've got Beth.'

'Mate, she's not going with you.'

'I'm not your mate.'

Shuffling, screaming and banging suggest a fight is going on. I only hope my new friends win.

'Get out,' yells Fred.

The front door slams then silence. I wait. I don't dare to breathe. Then footsteps up the stairs. I push myself further under the bed, praying if it's him he won't find me. The muffled footsteps get closer.

'Beth.' Lily. 'It's safe to come out now.'

I peer out from the side of the bed. 'Has he gone?'

'Yes, don't worry. We chucked him out.' I suspect Lily had nothing to do with it but I'm grateful for any help. Slowly I climb out, still shaking, still breathing so quickly that I worry I will pass out. I notice that Lily is trembling as well.

'Are you okay?' I ask.

'Yeah, fine.'

'Really?'

'Just reminded me of my ex. But we don't need to talk about that.'

'We can't stay here,' I say. Lily is obviously disappointed but nods. I am relieved that she hasn't decided to stay without me. 'Thank you,' I whisper.

'No problem,' she hugs me. 'We're a team. I wouldn't let you go by yourself.'

Fred and Steve are not happy.

'You almost got me killed,' shouts Fred dramatically. His face is red and I bet that by tomorrow he will have a black eye.

'I'm sorry.'

The tables by the door have been knocked over and the sofa has been pushed back. Even after everything that has happened I suddenly worry about Michael. What did they do to him? Is he alright?

'Get your stuff and go.'

'Whoa guys, calm down. We will go but we can't leave this minute. He could be out there waiting for us,' suggests Lily. I hadn't thought of that. My chest feels tight and I suddenly start to feel dizzy. 'We'll go later, right?'

'Fine,' answers Fred. 'Just make sure you're out by the morning.'

'Wait, maybe we should give them another chance,' Geri pipes up. Fred and Steve stare at her.

'Why should we do that?' asks Steve.

'Because she needs our help.' She points at me possessively.

'If you want to go with her, go,' says Fred. 'But she's not staying here.'

His word is final, Geri doesn't dare argue. I know the battle is lost.

We are leaving.

~

The rest of the evening is difficult. Fred and Steve throw me death stares. No one speaks, they don't ask questions, they don't care. When it gets dark, Lily and I pack our bags. We slink slowly out of the house, no goodbyes, no see you laters. We just go.

The darkness outside makes me more afraid of the area we're living in.

'Where are we going?' I whisper.

'I know a place.' She seems to know a lot of places. 'It's going to cost us though.'

'How much?'

'It's cheap but we can get jobs.'

I nod thinking it doesn't sound that easy. I've never had a job. I wouldn't even know where to start.

'Don't worry about it.'

'I'm not,' I answer quickly but I can tell she knows. She knows how I think.

'It all seems a nightmare right now but it'll get better I promise.' Ever the optimist, I have to smile.

Another bus ride, another town. The bedsit we arrive at seems even worse than the previous house and in an area as bad as the one we left but I am glad to be somewhere warm and away from men.

'I know it's not much,' offers Lily sadly. 'But it's what we can afford right now.'

'It's fine,' I say bravely. 'Like you say, we can get jobs and then we'll move up in houses and one day we'll have ourselves a mansion.' She laughs at this but you've got to dream right?

**September 2010**

The place we're living in reminds me of this holiday park we once stayed in when I was little: budget and pretty dirty. It was just Mum and Dad and me. Mum said we'd never go to such a place again. I remember the dust on the floor and Mum freaking out because I crawled over it, saying I was far too old to do such a thing, especially in a place like this. She immediately got out the disinfectant she'd bought with her and started cleaning up. I remember thinking 'what's the point of going on holiday just to clean up?' Now I wish Mum was here with her disinfectant. She'd hate me being in this place. I have been trying to ignore the mould on the walls, and the spiders in the corner are the least of my worries. I dread to think what is behind the dusty bed. I don't even want to peek.

The best thing here is the price. It is cheap and you can tell why. The landlady appears kind but I'm not feeling it. I don't know how anyone can let this out and live with themselves. She doesn't seem the most intelligent of people.

I have a job, a waitress at a local cafe. Okay I may have had to lie about my age and the pay is rubbish but it's enough. I could cry when I think about what I've lost but I am safe and I am free. Lily promises she will find a job too but it's not happened yet.

I smile at the customers as I serve them their tea and cakes. Jerry, the boss, is happy. He says I am prompt and quick and the customers like my smiley face. For some reason I get a buzz out of old ladies smiling back at me. They always make you feel like you are their granddaughter. They are probably craving love as well.

When I get back to the house, a man is arguing with the landlady.

'I want my money back.'

'That is not possible,' she replies in an accent which doesn't match her. She is clearly trying to make herself more posh.

'I am not staying here one more minute. I found a dead rat under the fridge.' The landlady shrugs, while I shiver at the thought. I hurry past, trying to shut my ears, but his voice is getting louder by the minute.

'My electricity has gone off three times, the whole place smells like a hippo's arse. I swear I've seen better refugee camps than this.'

I doubt he has ever seen a refugee camp but I don't feel it is my place to stop and argue. I get to our flat and lock the door behind me. I know the man is angry at her but he is making me feel scared nonetheless. I feel safer when I know I am in my locked apartment.

'You okay?' Lily is sat on the sofa, exactly where I left her this morning.

'That landlady is scaring me. Some guy is claiming he found a dead rat under the fridge.'

'Wouldn't surprise me in this place,' she chuckles.

I don't even want to look under the fridge to see if we have one. I didn't notice the smell before but now he's said it, it's all I can think about. *It's great,* I tell myself. *I'm free. I'm independent.* Tears roll down my cheeks. *It's fine.* But I know it's not. I don't want to be independent. I just want to be at home with Mum and Dad and Abby. I long for them more than I did before.

'Hey, it'll be okay,' Lily says, noticing my tears.

A knock at the door makes me jump up. 'Sorry about the shouting.' It is the landlady with a single flower, probably picked from the neighbour's lawn. She hands it to me. I take it carefully.

'Um, that's fine.'

'No, it's not. That man is crazy.' I only nod, not wanting to have this conversation. 'I mean imagine a rat under the fridge.' I don't want to imagine, thank you. 'I've never heard of anything so ridiculous. I find it quite insulting.'

I smile and start to edge the door closed. Her strange expression is starting to scare me and I am beginning to wonder if she is on drugs.

'Can I come in?'

'Um sorry but I'm just about to have a shower. I'm going out soon.' Her smile dips but she doesn't push it.

'Maybe another time.' Relieved, I watch her go and shut the door before she changes her mind.

'Psycho,' mutters Lily smirking.

Have I jumped from one bad situation to another?

A banging noise wakes me up in the middle of the night. In my sleepy state I can't work out what it is until I realise someone is knocking on our door. I am about to get up and answer it until I hear the landlady shouting.

'Get up bitch. Open the door. You don't turn me away!' She sounds drunk.

Oh crap, I'm in trouble now. I pull the duvet over me and put my hands over my ears until eventually the banging stops and she goes away. I don't sleep after that. I lay there wondering what the hell I'm doing with my life. One thing is for sure, we need to get out of here. But where? We can barely afford anything.

**October 2010**

'I need you both out by tomorrow.' The landlady is at the door, hands on her hips, staring at me intently.

'Why?' asks Lily, appearing behind me.

'Got someone else who's going to pay a lot more.' She says it with such disgust, like we are the scum of the earth for only paying what we do, despite the place being a hole.

'You can't do that,' argues Lily. 'You need to give us notice.'

'I am giving you notice. You've got till tomorrow. Besides, you have no contract.' She's right, we don't. We moved in such a rush that we didn't bother and we thought we wouldn't need one. I must admit though, I'm actually quite relieved. I hate this place.

'It's outrageous. I'm getting my lawyer on you,' shouts Lily as the landlady leaves. She laughs. I want to laugh too. Lily having a lawyer, what a joke! 'She can't do that to us. She is so out of order.'

'I know Lily but maybe it's for the best. This place is

horrible.' She looks hurt, I am insulting her choice of accommodation I suppose. 'Come on, you know it is.'

'Fine it is. It's disgusting but it's all we can afford.' I stop myself from having a go at her about getting a job. If she'd have got one we'd have more money by now, the little we've got is what I've earned.

'I'm sure there are other places out there.' She nods but I can see she doubts me.

'I'm going to pack and think about it.'

I leave it to her. I don't have a clue about that kind of stuff.

An hour later, I'm packed and sitting on the bed staring at the small bag with the little belongings I have when Lily bursts in.

'I've found some mates who will let us stay for a while. I rang them. They are happy to have us.'

Happy like Steve and Fred?

'Great.'

'Well, you don't have to sound so enthusiastic.'

'Sorry, I'm tired. I hate all this moving around.'

She throws her hands up in the air. 'What do you want Beth? I'm trying my best.'

'I know, I know. It's not your fault.'

'Go home if it's a problem.'

'No it's not. It'll be fine.' Her expression changes and a big smile comes across her face.

'Let's go then.'

As we leave, the landlady is outside her front door. She almost looks disappointed that we are going.

'You don't have to go until tomorrow.' We ignore her. She's not worth wasting any more words on. 'Or maybe you can stay if you pay a bit extra.'

'Can you believe her?' Lily exclaims when we are outside. 'Ridiculous woman, as if we'd want to stay in that shithole one minute longer.'

I don't point out that we were happy to stay in that dive until she made us go but that's beside the point.

'Onwards and upwards,' Lily announces cheerfully sounding like a posh TV show that my Mum used to watch.

Mum would be horrified if she could see where I'd been. She'd demand I come home right now. Dad, well who knows what he'd think. Happy one minute, angry the next.

We arrive at our next house after a long walk through town. I try to keep my head down, I am praying that no one I know will see us. 'Here it is,' announces Lily proudly as if it is a mansion. I must admit the house is big even if the area is not good. The front door is a typical council house door; white, PVC, with a tiny letterbox and a small frosted glass window in it. On the front lawn are piles of rubbish; bits of wood, an old toilet and an old mattress. The paint is peeling off the windows and there's a small crack below the roof. It's hardly got kerb appeal. It's the kind of house you would walk away from and never return to.

This is our new home.

The door is ajar as we approach, Lily pushes it.

'What are you doing?' I ask, horrified.

'Follow me.' She doesn't even seem to be bothered that someone might object to her entering without permission.

The whole house stinks as we enter and it's obvious what goes on here. I tentatively follow Lily as she marches in with confidence as if she owns the place. The residents, two men in their twenties, are sitting on the sofa, looking pretty out of it already.

'Hey, welcome!' shouts one. 'You must be Lily and- '

'Beth,' I finish.

'Hey Beth,' shouts the other one.

'Hi,' I answer shyly. I didn't expect them to be this friendly after Fred and Steve.

'I'm Charlie, this is Dave. Welcome to the madhouse.'

Here we go again. Is this what my life is going to be like, thrown from one dodgy house to the next?

# Part Three: After

## Beth - February 2018

Whispered frantic voices wake me from my fretful sleep. I take in the decor of my old bedroom and remember that I am home. I slowly ease my way out of bed to see what the fuss downstairs is about. I can hear what they are saying before I get there.

The voice that I recognise as the detective's voice echoes out to the corridor. 'That is my suggestion, Mr Kimmings.'

'We can't just run away.'

'Mr Kimmings, this isn't only one man. Michael is part of a wider network. Until we know the extent of it, your family is not safe.'

Abby stands behind me, scared. I throw her a little smile.

'It'll be okay,' I whisper. I take a deep breath and enter the lounge. They stop talking when they see me. 'What's going on?'

'We might need to get away for a while.'

I'm barely able to get the words out. 'This is my fault. I should have stayed away.'

Mum stands up quickly. 'No, no, of course you shouldn't. You did the right thing coming home.' What she says seems genuine but her tone tells a different story. Did they wish I was still missing rather than back at home causing trouble?

'Darling, you must never blame yourself for this,' says Dad. 'This is not your fault. It's that awful man, Michael.'

'We can arrange for somewhere safe for you if you would prefer,' suggests Detective Stevens.

'It's fine, I know somewhere we can go.'

Mum regards Dad's suggestion skeptically. 'You do?'

'I'll tell you about it later.'

'Well, I should get going.' Detective Stevens stands up and puts her coat on. 'Oh, one more thing. Beth, you mentioned a girl called Isabella?'

'Yes I did, why? She escaped. She went home.'

The detective sighs heavily. 'She didn't make it home. We have been through some records and I'm afraid I have some bad news. Isabella overdosed in March last year. Her parents hadn't seen her since she'd gone missing.'

Tears begin to pour down my face. The shock at hearing that Isabella is dead is too much.

'But Michael said she went home.'

'He was lying, sweetheart.' The detective's voice is sympathetic.

'She can't be dead.'

She takes out a piece of paper from her pocket. 'This was found in her possession. It's a letter she wrote to you seven years ago.'

I take it with a shaking hand. I barely notice Mum leading the detective out as I sink down onto the seat but I do notice Dad's unusually pale face staring at my hand. I stand up, taking the letter with me, to find a quiet place to read it. Dad doesn't move from his seat, it's like he's frozen to it.

I have to get to the privacy of my room before I lose it fully.

I shut the door firmly and lay on my bed and begin to read:

*Dear Beth,*

*I'm sorry for the trouble I caused you. I miss you so much and wish I could go back to living with you in that apartment. Even though the time we spent together was only short we became so close. You were a sister to me. No one else has cared about me like you did. Back then I thought it was awful but it was nothing compared to the new house I am in. They send me out every night to stand on street corners in the cold. I hope that no one will take me up on the offer but there is always one, far too many dirty old men around.*

*I wish I'd never run away. I wish I could go back home. One good thing is that I'm not pregnant. Thank goodness for that. I don't know how I would have dealt with that as well as all this.*

*Anyway, I am sending you this in the hope that you might one day rescue me. I don't know how but I can always hope.*

*Your friend and sister*

*Isabella*

That she never sent it hurts me deep inside. I'd like to think I would have come and found her if she had. Why did I believe Michael when he said that she had gone home? Why didn't I ask more questions? I throw the letter on my bed, tears streaming down my face. Mum enters the room and sits down next to me before I can object. She puts her arm around me.

'Are you okay?'

I lean my head on her shoulder.

'I'm sorry,' I whisper.

'Shssh. It's not your fault.' She strokes my hair.

'It is my fault. We got out but I persuaded her to go back and now she's dead. She said she hoped I would rescue her. Why didn't I?'

'Because you didn't know. You didn't know she was there.'

'But I should have looked harder.'

'Darling, none of this is your fault. You aren't responsible for what happened to your friend, and you aren't responsible for Michael being after us now.'

I look up doubtfully.

'You're not,' she says firmly. 'He manipulated you. You were just a kid.'

I nod. I know she's right but fifteen felt so old. I knew everything. I knew exactly what I wanted or so I thought. How wrong I was.

'Get your stuff packed, we're leaving tonight.'

'Tonight?'

'Yes, there's no point in hanging around here any

longer waiting for the next thing to happen. Your dad knows a house in the Lake District we can stay in.'

'The Lake District? But that's- '

'Miles away. I know. But that's good.'

'I suppose.'

'We'll be safe up there.'

'What about Abby going to school?'

'That's not important right now. We'll it figure out.'

I hug her tight. I never should have left.

~

The drive up north seems to take forever. I always knew the Lake District was high up on the map somewhere but I didn't quite realise how far up it was. The farthest North I had been before was a scummy bedsit in Derby two years ago. At least driving late at night we miss the traffic.

Abby sleeps next to me. She was so grumpy when she realised we were going away and possibly never coming back. I don't blame her. I would have felt the same at her age. Your friends and your social life is all that's important at that age. I try to tell her it'll be fun in the Lake District, what with the beautiful scenery, but it even sounds boring to me; stunning landscapes is not what you want aged fifteen.

At some point I must have fallen asleep because I awake to the sound of the car slowing down and we pull up outside a row of houses. It is dark, so dark that you can barely see in front of you. But we are here. And we are safe.

**Beth - December 2010**

'Beth get up!' Hands shaking me repeatedly.

I slowly open my eyes to see Charlie standing over me, panic written all over his face. 'What's up?'

'Men. Downstairs. Hide.'

Shit. I need to hide. My head is fuzzy, still hungover from last night's alcohol and drugs. I trip as I stumble out of bed and into the wardrobe. Charlie shuts me in.

'Where are you going?'

'I'll figure it out. Don't worry about me.' The door is barely shut when I hear voices, loud, in the room.

'Are they in here?' The sounds of them ransacking the place and then 'I'm taking these and anything you have for me.' Charlie mutters something indecipherable. I hold my breath, hoping it doesn't give me away. I should go out there and face the music, stand by my friend, but I am paralysed.

Shuffling sounds suggest that he is being taken away. I wait until the room is silent and I hear them troop down the stairs, the front door shuts. A car pulls away.

I am alone, finally.

I emerge to an empty house that's been torn apart. Damn, another place I need to move on from. My hands tremble from shock and withdrawal. I raid the kitchen cupboards for what is left of the food we had and stuff it into my backpack.

As I leave the house, Lily climbs out of the coat cupboard.

'Hey, you made it too,' she laughs. I grab her hand and help her out.

'Come on, we have to get out of here.'

'Oh but I'm so tired.' She sways from side to side. Maybe not the burden I need but she helped me when I had no one, it is the least I can do.

'And I could really do with more- '

'I know a secret stash.' She has a cheeky grin on her face.

'Have you not noticed, they ransacked the place?'

'Not this hiding place.' She goes into the lounge and carefully takes the picture of the forest that I've always found calming, and dumps it on the floor, creating a big rip along the side of it in the process. Behind it is a small hole where I can see plastic bags poking out.

'You're a genius.'

'I am totally a genius,' she says proudly, as she throws me a bag. 'Get this in you and let's get out of here.'

**Beth - February 2018**

The little white house is tucked away behind a whole row of others. I would have preferred it if it had been completely isolated.

'No one will disturb us here,' says Dad. 'Nothing but a few hardy walkers here at this time of year.'

I glance at Abby uneasily who smiles in return as if to reassure me, the previous day's tension gone. I have to admit the surroundings are making us feel calmer already. Mountains border the house on all sides, the tops of the tallest one is invisible beneath the thick white clouds. The trees, naked of their leaves, sway heavily in the cold wind. The opposite mountain side is green and mossy, not unlike a snooker table. A couple of cottages are dotted at the bottom. Part of the summit is illuminated where the sun is breaking through the cloud, desperate to get out. I can relate to that.

Even though we are so far away I still don't feel free, in fact I feel more trapped than ever before. At twenty two I should be living in the world not hiding away in the North West with my parents and my teenage sister. Guilt washes over me when I see Abby solemnly slumped on the picnic bench, wrapped up in her coat and scarf, ready to wage war on her parents and anyone else who dares come near. I brought this upon them.

'Right guys, after we've unpacked we can play a board game.'

Abby's look of disdain says it all. It says *we're not five, Dad.* I smile encouragingly at him. The good thing about staying here is we have no signal: no one can contact me, no one can hassle me.

Five minutes later Dad pokes his head out of the front door. 'Board game?'

Abby doesn't move.

'Couldn't we … you know … go and explore. I could take Abby and leave you both in peace.'

Abby perks up, hope in her eyes.

Dad looks disappointed but I also sense a bit of relief in there.

'Take care of her and don't get lost.'

'I promise,' I call but we are already through the gate and halfway down the hill.

'Thanks,' says Abby as I avoid yet another crunchy cow pat. 'I wasn't in a board game mood.'

'Me neither.'

We follow the field to the bottom where there is a stone stile to climb over and a public footpath sign pointing in between two cottages.

'I'm sorry about this,' I say.

Abby shrugs. 'It's no big deal.'

'No, it is. I've ruined our lives.'

Abby stops and grabs my shoulder. 'You haven't ruined our lives. Michael has.'

'But if it wasn't for me being stupid.'

'Beth if an older man had come on to me I'd have been out of here too. An older man or staying with your boring parents? I know what I would have chosen.'

'How did you get to be so wise?'

She shrugs. We continue on in silence as the path narrows into the woods, only separated from neighbouring cottages by a wall of stones that looks like someone had just stacked up a minute ago. Eventually the path opens up into the forest and through the bare trees you can make out Lake Bassenwaithe, surrounded by mountains.

'It's beautiful huh?'

Abby smiles in agreement. 'Do you think we could swim in it?'

'Are you mad? It's February.'

We settle with paddling. The rocks make it difficult to paddle far without feeling you'd lose your balance and after a minute my toes feel like they are going to freeze off. I glance around nervously to see if anyone is here but it is mostly deserted except for an old couple with two dogs, who look bigger than their owners, and a young couple taking romantic selfies of themselves by the lake. Envy flashes through me. It could have been me and Michael - it's how it should have been. I miss someone loving me that much.

'Don't think about him,' Abby says. 'He's not worth it.'

'You're right.' How can she understand? How can anyone understand when I don't even know why I have these feelings myself. What stupid person could still love someone after what he'd put me through? But outsiders would fail to see the complicated feelings I feel: I love him yet hate him; I need him, I want him, yet I fear him; I yearn for him still, I long to jump on the next train back home and find him. How can I explain that?

It makes no sense even to me.

'So Beth, if you escaped after a few months- '

'Quite a lot of months, but anyway. '

'Why didn't you come home then?'

I sigh 'It's- '

'If you are going to say complicated, don't bother.'

'The truth is I thought Mum and Dad might not want me back.'

'Why wouldn't they? They've been pining for you for years. Mum never got over it.'

'I can see that now but I was worried that they would hate me for running away.'

'Beth, nobody could hate you.' She puts her arm around me which makes me want to cry. 'So where did you go?'

'I went to a women's refuge to start with, then I lived in various flats, some good, some not so good.' I don't want to talk about this now but she seems happy with that answer.

'I'm glad you did come home.'

~

Two days into our extended Lake District stay and already the rain is starting to get to me. This place is beautiful and the mountains take my breath away, but it rains so much. A mist descends over the mountain tops, making it disappear. A sense of isolation overwhelms me and I long for a bustling big town. I have to get out despite the rain. I have to or I'll go crazy.

I step out into the rain, ignoring Mum's protests that I'll be soaked through. I don't care. The rain is coming down so hard my trousers are instantly wet. My rain mac protects my upper body but that's as far as it goes. I step onto the grass to cross the field, I ignore the soggy feeling it leaves me with in my shoes. I squelch down to the bottom of the field. The rain and wind are so strong I don't hear Abby creeping up behind me.

'How did you get out?'

'Past the terminator, Mum you mean?'

'Ha, yes.'

'I ran out of the door. I think she'd given up at this point. Told me I was mad and would regret it later.'

'I think I'm regretting it already,' I say shivering, feeling the cold right through to my bones.

'It's that or Scrabble.' I laugh. Dad seems to have developed an obsession with Scrabble in the last few days. The rest of us hate it. He comes up with these obscure words that no one's heard of. When he's not beating us at Scrabble, he seems to be out a lot. He says he's going to the shop to buy food but then he comes back with nothing, murmuring about not having what we wanted. Sometimes I fail to understand him. I suppose seven years changes people. He seems different to me now but I was only a kid back then. Maybe I just viewed it differently.

## Beth - May 2010

'Go on, you go in.' I throw Lily a reluctant glance before stepping forward into the restaurant. The waiter looks at me as if I am a homeless vagrant, which isn't far from the truth I admit. I give him my most winning smile.

'Hi there.' He frowns and doesn't return the smile. 'I was wondering if you had any jobs going?'

He raises his eyebrows and says quickly 'No, I'm sorry.'

'Are you the manager?' He shakes his head as he tries to go back to polishing glasses. 'Can I speak to him?'

'*She* is not here and I know for a fact that there are no jobs.'

'Thank you for your time,' I say, pasting a fake smile on my face. I walk out with my head held high. I didn't need his stupid job.

When I return, Lily is full of hope 'Well?'

I shake my head.

'We're never going to get a job.'

'Are you surprised? We look like homeless druggies.'

'That's because we are homeless druggies,' she laughs.

'Maybe we should go clean first.' She looks at me like I have gone mad, like I am the craziest person alive. 'Just a suggestion,' I say, waving my arm at her.

We walk down to the riverfront. It's beautiful when the sun is shining. I am hopeful. Hopeful that I can make a life again. The last two years since I escaped from Michael have been a rollercoaster ride of different houses with different people. I have sunk to the lowest depths, been sat on the street ready to die. But Lily always keeps me going. She pulls me up, literally, and tells me I have to carry on. She struggles as much as I do. That's what makes her special.

She needs me; I need her.

'Hey, I've got an idea,' she says as we are staring at the passing tourist boat. 'We could do that.'

'Do what?'

'Be tour guides, like that one.' She points to the American lady, who's voice can be heard for miles, standing on the side of the boat. I am doubtful and smile uneasily at her. I can't imagine anyone wanting to employ us to be guides for rich tourists.

'Come on.' She leaps up and drags me by the hand. Another one of her hair brain schemes. What have we got to lose?

The Irish man selling the tickets for the boat gives us a cheeky grin.

'You really think you could do that?' he asks with an accent to die for.

'Of course we can,' says Lily confidently.

He laughs. 'But only if you get new clothes. You look like you just stepped out of Les Miserables.'

I am laughing too much to be insulted.

'If you give us an advance we can do that.' She is cheeky but it works as he hands us £50.

'Don't spend it all at once.'

We dance away to the nearest Primark.

'Can you believe it? I got us a job.'

'Unbelievable. Thanks Lily. I owe you one.' I don't add *again* but it feels like that. If anyone was keeping a tally of the favours Lily had done me it would outweigh what I had done for her by far.

'You mean the world to me.' She strokes my cheek.

To anyone passing by you'd think we were lovers, but that's not what it is. We are like sisters. We may not be related but she is the best I have.

**Abby - March 2018**

I must admit, the idea of climbing a mountain was not one that was appealing to me but here we are. Three days in and I find myself balanced on a rock, trying desperately to get across to more slippery rocks and somehow we're not even close to the top.

'Come on Abby, put your foot there,' Beth says encouragingly. When did she become so good at giving instructions? Today I have learnt that Beth is a good person to have when you are stuck halfway up a mountain. Her soothing voice reassures me. When I finally manage to get across I try not to think about the return journey.

'See, said you could do it.'

'Thanks Beth.'

Apparently Barf's not a big mountain; it's one of the smaller ones. I dread to think what it would be like climbing a big one. The steepness of it is tiring but I feel a sense of achievement every step I take, not that I would admit that to Mum. After everything that's happened we are here, alive, climbing a mountain. And yes, this place is amazing. Again, don't tell Mum. I keep glancing out of the window just to see that view. I can't imagine ever getting tired of it. I feel an wonderful sense of peace here and everything seems good again.

We might actually get through this.

Dad has been very distant since we got here. I mean he's making an effort, trying to persuade us to play board games and the like, but I can tell his hearts not in it. I am almost glad when he goes out to find a signal, he does have a business to run still I guess. He is pretty snappy, getting grumpy about every little thing we say. Even Mum can't say the right things without earning a look of disgust. I wonder if they will get a divorce when this is over. They don't seem very happy anymore. I wish we had a happy family but I'm not sure that family has existed for a very long time. For now I'm grateful that we are protected from danger and that creep Michael isn't after us.

I'm getting really tired on this "small" mountain when Beth's voice sounds loud and clear. 'Come on Abby we're almost at the top.' She is lying, I know it. I've heard about false peaks but I need her encouragement. I press on up the wet ground, telling myself I can do this. Despite the effort, I feel alive and happy out here in nature.

Finally we reach the top and the view is virtually obscured by the cloud descending over us.

'Typical, can't see a bloody thing,' says Dad grumpily.

'At least we got to the top,' I reply. 'My first ever mountain.' It's hard to hide the pride I am feeling.

'Well done, you did amazingly,' replies Mum beaming at me.

'So apparently,' begins Beth, 'this mountain is named Barf because of the Bishop of Barf.'

'How do you know that?' I ask.

'I searched it up before we started with the tiny bit of signal that I managed to get. According to legend, the bishop of Barf made a drunken bet that he could ride his horse up this mountain, drunk.'

'What an idiot,' I comment.

Dad pipes up. 'I agree.'

'So what happened to him?' Mum asks, desperate to know.

'Well he died, of course. He was drunk riding a horse up a mountain - who wouldn't fall and die doing that?'

'Oh I kind of hoped he made it,' adds Mum.

I stare at her incredulously. 'Really?'

She shrugs and laughs. 'I'm ever the hopeful one.'

'Or naïve,' mutters Dad.

'What did you say?' Mum says sharply.

'Nothing.' She stares at him but he turns away.

I will her to leave it because we are having such a nice day and I don't want anything to spoil it but the comment has clearly angered her. What exactly did he mean by that anyway?

I thought going down would be the easy bit but halfway back my knees and feet are starting to kill me and I haven't forgotten the dangerous ridge across the water that I will have to scramble across again. I end up scooting down it on my bottom. I don't care that I am getting muddy or that this is the second set of clothes I have got wet today. The gravel is slippery and the rain begins to fall quite heavily. Luckily our macs serve us well and keep some part of us dry.

We are relieved when we get to the bottom.

'I hope you've bought hot chocolate,' I say.

'Of course. When would I ever forget that.'

Fortunately it's a quick hop across the road and our cottage is there. We are happy to feel the warmth of it and the opportunity to get dry. I dump my wet clothes on the ever increasing pile by the washing machine, wishing I'd bought more.

'Don't leave them there!' Mum yells.

'I wasn't going to,' answers Beth angrily.

'Whoa, sorry.'

'No I'm sorry. I didn't mean to snap. It's just- '

'Just what?'

'I had a flat mate in one of the places I lived that was very nagging, constantly having a go at me. Nothing I did was good enough. Sorry, you're not like her at all.'

She joins me in our bedroom, shutting the door before Mum can ask any questions. There is a lot I want to ask but don't. She's had so many experiences away from us. What else has she gone through that we don't know about?

As I step outside the bedroom, Dad is leaving.

'Where are you going?' Mum asks.

He glances back at her with a cryptic expression. 'I need to find Wi-Fi to do some work.'

'I thought you were done for the day.'

'Your work is never done being self-employed. I won't be long.' He leaves before Mum can argue with him. She stares at the space where he stood.

I want to run after him, hug him, and tell him I love him and ask him why he can't be the father I so love.

'Hot chocolate?' Mum asks with a small smile.

'Yes please. I'm freezing.'

## Beth - March 2017

'Come on, Lily. It's our first day.' I am brimming with excitement at the thought of being tour guides on that little boat on the Thames. We're going to have money and dignity. Lily is still asleep so I push her to one side to try and jolt her into reality.

'Come on, we're going to be late.'

'No, too tired. You go without me.'

'Don't be silly, you got us these jobs.' She opens her eyes and then I know that she's had too much.

'Lily, what have you done?' But I can see exactly what from the stash next to her. She stares at me with a glazed expression. I've never seen her like this. Usually she's up and ready for anything the next day, whatever has happened the night before. 'Lily you're scaring me.' She closes her eyes and rolls over and I know we're in trouble.

I start to pace. What should I do? Do I call an ambulance? Do I leave her and hope that she'll be okay? Should I go and explain to Patrick why we can't work today? I can't think straight. I shove her again but no response, not even a groan.

'Damn it,' I say pulling out my phone. I call an ambulance.

They are here within half an hour, not bad for a Saturday morning. Surely they must have more important patients than an overdosed druggie.

'What has she taken?' But they look around they know, they shake their head at me, probably wanting to know why I let her take them.

'We're going to take her to hospital. Do you want to come in the ambulance?' I nod. Our job will have to wait, if we still have a job. I hate to think that he is standing there, waiting for us, thinking that we have done a runner on him with our new clothes.

I'm not allowed to go in with her but have to sit in the

waiting room, as far away from everyone else as I can. I jiggle my legs up and down nervously. I want to get out of here.

'Any news?' I ask the receptionist after an hour's wait.

'Are you family?'

'Technically, no, but we're like family.' I can see from her face that's not good enough.

'Unless you're family I can't tell you anything but I'll tell her parents you are here.'

'Her parents?' She points at a middle aged couple standing by the door. She has parents? Well of course she has. Why should I be surprised? Part of me wants to run away, the other part wants to find out if she's alright. I decide to be brave and approach them.

'Hi I'm Beth. Lily's friend. Is she okay?' Her mother's face is hostile at the sight of me, my bedraggled hair and falling apart clothes do nothing to endear me to her.

'She's fine, no thanks to you.' I want to tell her that Lily is always the one to get the drugs. She gives them to me, not the other way round. 'She's coming home with us now.' She walks away before I can say any more.

'Thank you for asking,' adds her Dad, with a softer expression, his small voice barely heard, if it were my Dad everyone would know about it.

Alone again. Lily is gone. No job, no friend. Hopeless once more.

**Abby - March 2018**

I am so bored. I never thought I'd say this, but I am missing school. Anything would be better than spending more quality time with my dumb family up a mountain. I get that it's beautiful and everything but I'm not fifty. I should be doing something exciting with my life. I'm going to die of boredom up here. Climbing mountains was a novelty to start with but now it's getting so old.

I go out for yet another walk down the hill, trying to

avoid the gross cow pats. Seriously, I have spent so much time flicking bits of cow shit off my shoes with tiny sticks.

I follow the familiar path towards the lake, anything to get out of that house. When I check my phone there is a message on Instagram. I'm amazed I have signal and even more so that someone would DM me.

*Hey there, I'm Harry from next door. I saw you move in. Don't get many kids round here. Do you want to hang out sometime?*

Finally, excitement in my life.

*Sure, where and when?*

*You free now? I'm in the forest bit at the end of the field.*

Usually there is virtually no one around but there he is, a rather fit man, dressed in a soft fleecy top, sitting by the tree. He could be in his twenties but I'm not sure. He smiles at me as I approach.

'Hi.' He has a smile that melts my heart.

'Hi,' I reply shyly. Suddenly I have no idea what to say.

'Haven't seen you round here before.'

'No … we just got here.' Inside my head I am cursing myself, I'm an idiot. What do I sound like?

'I'm staying with my Nan,' he adds. 'Before I go to university in a few months.' University! He must be younger than I'd thought. 'Do you want to walk with me to the lake?'

I nod enthusiastically, hoping I don't seem too keen. I don't want him to think I'm desperate, although really I am. I am craving something a bit exciting round here.

~

I am in love. His name is Harry. Even his name is gorgeous. He has the most adorable blue eyes. I could stare into them every minute of the day. By the time we have walked along the lake for half an hour I have found out so much about him. I feel I have known him forever. Of course, I have told him the edited version of my life. I am not that stupid to put our family in danger again. He doesn't need to know the gory details. He is going to study Psychology at university but he's taken a few months out to mind his Nan who is ill. I mean how adorable is that? He is so cute.

When I wander back to the cottage, I am on cloud nine or more like nine hundred and nine. Beth quizzes me the minute I get in; even she can tell I'm different. 'You look happy?'

'Was a good walk,' I say slyly.

'A good walk?'

'Yeah, you know, cleared my mind.'

'Oh right.' She regards me strangely. She clearly doesn't believe me.

I lay on my bed and stare up at the ceiling. Already I am imagining a life with Harry and his boyish grin and floppy hair. How will I cope when he goes to university? What will I do when we go back home? Maybe we should get married. No that's crazy, we just met. Who would marry someone they just met? But he's so adorable.

~

I don't have to wait long to see Harry again. The next day he messages me.

*You free to meet?*

*Absolutely.*

*You know where?* I run there before he can change his mind.

He smiles broadly at me and I feel like my heart will break, it is so full. His face is slightly red as if he's been on a run.

'Hey, do you want to go for a different walk today? I know of another path.'

'Sure.' I trust him, of course I do. I haven't told anyone who I'm with. Mum and Dad wouldn't understand. They would freak out if they knew I was meeting a boy. Mum especially would have some bizarre idea that history was going to repeat itself. I mean what's the likelihood of meeting another dodgy older man so far from home? He's fine, he totally is.

He takes me on a magical mystery tour. Suddenly the

scenery has taken on new meaning for me. As we walk he tells me facts about the different types of trees. He knows so much.

'You didn't say what you were doing? College, uni?'

Of course he assumes I am older, why wouldn't he.

'I'm at sixth form college,' I lie.

'Cool. Do you enjoy it?'

'Most of the time,' I laugh. It needs to sound realistic. 'Physics is my favourite subject.' Why did I say that? I can't stand any kind of Science.

'Heavy stuff.'

I can't believe the extent of my own lies.

'What do you want to do when you leave?'

Damn, now I have to sound like a girl with a plan. If I say I don't know he will think I am just bumbling through life aimlessly.

'I want to be a Physics lecturer at a university,' I say suddenly. It is the first intelligent job I can think of. My friend's dad at school, a grey old man, is one. I wish now I had chosen a career for someone less than eighty but Harry seems impressed and nods approvingly.

**May 2017**

*I can see you standing there, head held high, dressed up smart. You think you're safe. You think I've moved on.*

*You wait for the interview, hands twitching, fiddling, clearly nervous but confident. I've seen you go from deflated, worthless, to someone who's trying to make a go of life. You seem to have given up the drugs and certainly those druggie friends. You've even found a few decent ones. You live in that high rise flat, it's a bit cheap but it's a long way from that drug house you were in. You think I don't know where you are but I do. I will always be able to find you.*

*You enter the building, hope in your eyes, clutching your bag. When you appear half an hour later you have happiness written all over your face. Did you get that job, darling? Do you think it's that easy to move on?*

*You walk quickly away. You meet him again.*

*That boy is far too nice for you with his baby face, I bet he doesn't know your past or that you used to sleep with lots of men. He takes your hand with an air of possession. Don't get used to it, he won't last. You walk lightly without a care in the world but I know you.*

*He takes you to a cafe; it's hardly Marchello's is it? Do you miss those days when you wore beautiful dresses and were adored by many? You've put on weight since then. It doesn't suit you.*

*I see the way you laugh when he talks to you. What could he possibly say that is so funny? You never laughed with me in that way. Why so happy?*

*I guess I should be glad you're making a go of it but I've lost control of you and I hate that. It makes me feel inadequate; didn't I do a good enough job with you? None of this is because of me. I'm the one who should be sorting out your life. I'm the one you should turn to when you're in trouble, not him.*

*Don't get contented with this life. It'll change before you know it. I'll get you back.*

*I'll find a way.*

**Beth - March 2018**

Abby seems unusually happy.

She has gone from grumpy teenager to this light and airy person who is acting like someone in love.

Oh my goodness she is in love. No, she can't be. How can she be? We are living in the middle of nowhere. But she is like me when I met Michael. What if she's met someone like Michael? I have to protect her.

Wait, I can't rush in. She'll freak out. I would have. First I need proof. Maybe she is happy and accepting life here. No, no way. Abby is not the kind of person to accept something without good reason. I am slowly getting to know more about her since I moved back in, especially being here, so close together. I am learning that she is very stubborn. I guess not unlike the eight-year-old I left.

I watch her like a hawk. She smiles a lot, more than normal. She is putting on more makeup (I mean what's the point up here?). She is being nice to everyone. That afternoon she announces she is going for a walk.

'I'll come,' I say jumping up quickly.

'Oh no, er … I'd rather go on my own.'

'Oh,' I say feigning hurt.

'It's not that I don't like your company, it's only I want to be on my own.' She looks terrified that she has upset me. I try to resist laughing.

'It's fine. I'll stay here then.' I pretend to be annoyed. She skips out of the house, she is literally dancing on air. I wait a few minutes after the front door shuts before I get up.

'I thought you were staying here?' says Mum peering up from her book.

'I'm going on my own walk.'

~

I can just about see her at the bottom of the field climbing over the stile. Quickly I run to the wall and hide in true stealth mode, feeling like a spy. I peep up and see her heading down towards the lake.

When she is out of sight I run down the hill not caring that I have stepped in about three cow pats. When I reach the bottom and have climbed over the stile myself, I peer slowly around the cottage.

I don't see her so I carry on along the path leading to the forest. When I reach the end I spot her under a tree with a man. I knew it. He must be slightly older than me. Dark, handsome, slight stubbly beard - who wouldn't fall in love with him? But seriously, what a pervert!

I watch them from a distance. Abby's body language is all over him, leaning towards him, flicking back her hair, laughing. Was I the same with Michael I wonder? I cringe, to think I might have been as embarrassing as Abby. After a few minutes chatting they wander off, hand in hand, towards the lake. He's not that much taller than Abby. I follow them but watch from a distance.

Half an hour later she walks back alone, like she is floating on air.

'Hey you,' I say, jumping out from behind a tree. 'Who was that?'

She seems surprised and slightly guilty 'Who was who?'

'Don't play dumb with me. "Mr, oh I'm so good looking" who you went for a walk with.'

'Have you been following me?' Her eyes narrowing in anger.

'I wanted to make sure you were okay.'

'Being nosy more like.'

'So who is he?'

Her expression softens. 'Harry. He's staying with his Nan while taking a year out from university.'

'University? But he must be about 25.'

'He's 18.'

'What? He told you that?'

'Yes he did. He is 18.'

'Oh seriously Abby! There is no way that he is 18. He is lying to you.'

'What do you know about it?'

I fling my arms up in the air. 'What do I know? Do you really need to ask that?'

'This is different.' She raises an eyebrow at me in answer. 'Of course. He's not a bad man. I'm not an idiot.'

Her words grate on me. 'Like me you mean?'

'I didn't mean that.'

'Oh yeah, of course you didn't. You all think I'm an idiot for getting involved with a man like Michael.'

'We do not and I'm not about to make the same mistake. Stop being so overprotective. I'm allowed to have a boyfriend. Just leave me alone.'

I watch as she storms up the hill, leaving me seething and anxious. I don't want history to repeat itself. Maybe I am being paranoid. I mean, we are far away from Michael. He can't have found us. No one knows we are here, and what are the chances of this Harry being the same?

When I reach the cowpat field Abby is sitting on the wall at the top of it. I am breathless when I reach her but I manage a smile.

'I'm sorry,' I say. 'I know you're sensible. I worry about you.'

'You do and I appreciate that but I'm not eight anymore.'

We sit in silence for a few minutes staring up at the ever darkening sky as the clouds begin to close in.

'Are you going to tell Mum and Dad?'

'About what?'

'About Harry.'

'No way. They'll go mad like you did.'

'True.' I smile. I know she's right. Mum especially is very sensitive right now. She won't be able to cope with the idea of another one of her daughter's having an older man. 'Be careful Abby. Don't run away or anything.'

'I wouldn't do that, I'm not- '

'I know; I know, stupid like me.'

She smiles sympathetically at me. I will just have to keep an eye on them.

## June 2017

*I see he got my note, that nice boy of yours. Judging by his expression as he walks quickly away, bag packed, face determined. I guess he didn't know about your dark past. He's too young for you. He obviously can't handle the truth.*

*You don't leave the house for days. Did you think he was the one? He was far too fickle. You don't need him.*

*When you finally leave, you look awful. Have you given in to drugs again? Tut tut, you just can't stay clean can you? You think you can move on but it isn't easy is it?*

*What happened to that nice little job of yours? I see you creep in there, guiltily; you know you haven't been a perfect employee. It's a tough world out there. Merely five minutes later you are kicked out.*

*It doesn't take long to get sacked, does it? What will you do now? The hopelessness is returning to your eyes. You won't last out there on your own.*

*You try to carry on but there's internal struggle in your eyes. You so badly want to be taken care of you again, don't you? You must be missing that life of luxury you had for so long.*

*Your neighbours are beginning to give you "looks" -you know the kind that people give when they disapprove of you. They know something is not right.*

*You don't seem to notice; too pumped full of alcohol and drugs I suspect.*

*Then the unthinkable happens, you leave that apartment of yours. What, you thought money would just grow on trees and allow you to live there without a job?*

*You trudge along the pavement, shoulders slumped, hair out of place, bag on your back, the only belongings you have in the world. Why don't you go home? It must have occurred to you but you're too stubborn, aren't you? You won't admit that you need help.*

*Exhausted, you sit by a shop, homeless yet again. You lay your head against the glass door, night draws in, and it's still cold out there. Passers-by barely give you a glance, don't think to stop and help. They wouldn't believe it was the same person if they'd seen you before.*

*Finally you move and take yourself into a cafe and buy a drink with the little money you have, ignoring the waiter's disdainful manner. He's seen your kind before. But you have money, so he can't refuse you, not yet anyway. It's only a matter of time before you run out - then what? Have you even got a plan?*

*You drink in silence, head down, full of shame and sadness. My little princess, it didn't have to come to this. If only you had stayed where you were supposed to. You need someone to take care of you.*

*Don't worry, help is coming. You won't have to survive for long. You may have rejected me before but I won't give up on you. You see, I'm faithful. People may not like the way I do things but I never let those I love down.*

*Watch and wait, help is coming.*

*You leave. I don't see where you go. I can't watch anymore. It's too painful, too tempting to come and rescue you now. But you wouldn't understand. It's better this way.*

*You'll see.*

**Abby - April 2018**

'How about we go out for the day?' Mum asks hopefully at breakfast. I raise my eyebrows at her. I had hoped to meet Harry, but it appears he is busy.

'Too dangerous?' I suggest, hoping she will agree.

'No one knows we're here. It'll be fine,' she replies.

'No, she's right,' comments Dad, 'far too dangerous.' I didn't expect him to back me up.

'Don't be ridiculous,' she says. 'We are safe here.'

'We're never safe,' Dad adds dramatically, sending a shiver down me.

'Don't be melodramatic, Jack, you're scaring Abby.'

He gets up aggressively. 'I'm being melodramatic?' he shouts. 'You're the one that's spent the last seven years crying.'

'That is low, Jack.' Mum stands up to face him. They are like two gorillas ready to fight. Beth and I stare at each other.

Mum backs away and decides to leave before she does something she'll regret. If we hadn't been there it would have been a lot worse but I can see she doesn't want to upset us. I find her in the bedroom moving clothes around aimlessly.

'I don't mind going out,' I say, hoping to cheer her up. She smiles weakly at me. 'We can go in your car.'

'I'm not sure if anyone else wants to.'

'Beth does. Don't know about Dad but we could always go without him.'

'Let's do it. Where do you want to go?'

'Somewhere with civilisation?' she laughs. We'd all like a bit of that right now.

~

Fortunately the rain holds off as we head to Whinlatter Country Park.

Dad, as expected, decides to bail out on us, saying he has work to do. Fine with us, we're happier without him these days.

The road leading up to the country park gets steeper and steeper and I wonder where we'll end up. It's unlike any country park down south.

'Can't we for once go to a place without steep hills?' I ask.

Beth laughs.

'This is the Lake District. What did you expect?'

I shrug grumpily.

'Look, there's a Gruffalo walk.'

'I'm not a kid,' I retort.

'No really! You've never told me that before.'

I stick my middle finger up at Beth.

'Abby!' Mum exclaims in shock but laughs anyway. I think Mum is just glad we're out and about and enjoying life. We scramble through the woody paths before retiring to the cafe for a well-earned hot drink. We can barely feel our toes and our fingertips are ready to fall off. but the warmth of the cafe sucks us in.

We didn't tell Dad where we were going so I'm surprised to see him walk past.

Mum gets up to run to the door but then quickly returns.

'Where's Dad?'

'Oh he had already gone by the time I'd got there.' We don't question it further but continue sipping our very hot drinks. I wonder what Dad is doing here.

When we get home I express my fears to Beth.

'Don't you think it's weird that Dad was at the country park? I mean what "business" would take him there?'

She shrugs. 'I have no idea, Abby,' she answers wearily. 'Maybe he was meeting a business associate there.'

'A business associate?' I say with raised eyebrows.

She laughs. 'I don't know.'

I can see I'm not getting anywhere with Beth so I leave her in our bedroom. I'm twitchy. I can't sit still. Something isn't right. I find myself in Mum and Dad's bedroom. I don't know what I'm doing there, trying to find clues maybe. About what though I'm not sure. It's a good job Dad's out as he would freak to see me rifling through his drawers. It's mostly full of the usual things you'd expect to find in a bedside drawer; paracetamols, tweezers and an old photo of Mum from when she was younger.

I am about to give up when I stumble upon an envelope addressed to someone called Freddie but with our address on it. Without thinking I open it. It's an official looking letter on headed paper which appears to indicate it was written by a professional counsellor, but the content seems anything but official.

*Dear Freddie,* it begins, *I haven't heard from you in a while. You missed your last appointment. I am worried about you. We still have a lot to talk about. Please call me. Yours sincerely Peter Griffths.*

Who is Freddie? Why was this person writing to him at our address? And why does Dad have this letter?

Before I can ponder the questions anymore, I hear Dad's voice downstairs. I quickly put the letter back in the envelope and carefully return it before leaving the bedroom.

~

'We went to Whinlatter country park,' I can hear Mum telling Dad as I am halfway down the stairs. I study his face to judge his reaction. If he is feeling panicky he doesn't show it. He doesn't say he was there too but maybe he had a genuine reason to be there.

That evening, as we enjoy a meal thrown together from leftovers, laughter fills the room. Life seems sweet for a few hours. I don't think about the past. I don't think about the future. For now I am grateful that we are together again.

'So this man was standing there sweeping and sweeping. I swear his arms must have been getting tired,' I giggle as Beth speaks.

'Huh what?' Mum seems to tune back into the conversation.

'Mum, do you listen to a word I say?'

'Sorry Beth, just thinking.'

'She was talking about the weird old man down the road.'

'Abby, it's not nice to call people weird.'

'It is when they are,' laughs Dad.

'Jack, you are such a bad example,' Mum laughs back. They are suddenly like a young couple in love. He puts his hand through the bit of hair that he has left and smiles naughtily. I don't even want to know what that means, though I suspect I do.

'You'll be a weird old man one day, Dad,' comments Beth.

'He already is,' I respond cheekily.

'Oi! I am not that old.' Mum gives him a look which casts doubt on that. Not that old. Anyone over forty is ancient.

'Right, I'm going for a walk,' I announce as soon as I have shovelled in my last mouthful.

'Again?'

'Yes, Mum, again. You always say we don't get enough exercise.'

'You can't go on your own. It's getting dark.'

'I'll go with her,' offers Beth. I try to throw her off with a death stare but I shrug. I give up. She can come if she wants to.

'Fine.'

The sun is setting as we walk down the hill, wrapped in our scarves, the cottages silhouetted against the sky, idyllic like a painting.

## July 2017

*I see you've met Simon then. I told you help was coming. He's an attractive man isn't he? Obviously not as handsome as me, but who can be.*

*It didn't take much for you to fall for him at the cafe. You're lucky he looked twice at you the way you're dressed at the moment. You seem to have lost all sense of style, maybe you just don't care.*

*He marched in, full of suave and style. Deep down you love that kind of thing don't you? Your face full of smiles, he brought a sparkle to you again; I've missed seeing that. See, I told you that you would be happier without that boy. You are proud to be around Simon and you know the best thing? I don't have to follow you around anymore. He reports back to me, tells me everything. It won't be long before you are back on the circuit again, you were quite the little earner and I have to say business could be better right now.*

*He asked you to move in with him, he told me you jumped at the chance. You're a fool if you can't see what's happening. He reckons you're in love with him. You don't learn do you? But you're safe now. You're off the streets. He'll take care of you. Restore you to your former self, pretty dresses and fancy restaurants.*

*I'm sure you've missed that.*

*He says you love the new dress I suggested he buy for you. I know your style. Simon doesn't have a clue. Despite him being all lovey and charming, he needs a lot of guidance. I can see you now in his expensive apartment, standing in front of his mirror admiring yourself in the new dress with his eyes devouring you with every look.*

*I can't resist a sneaky peek at you as you leave his apartment. I know, I know, I said I would leave the spying to Simon now but I can't resist. You are stunning, ready to go out to dinner, and so much younger. You've finally come off the drugs. It makes a difference. The haunted look in your eyes has gone, they are shining again. I knew Simon was the right one for you. He's taking care of you, I said he would.*

*I watch as he guides you into his car. I don't suppose you notice his sports car but it's a privilege he wouldn't have without me. It's your favourite colour isn't it? Red, like that dress you looked stunning in. Your smile is enough to light up any room. Simon glances around proudly and why shouldn't he? He has a beautiful girl with him.*

*I made you. I created you the way you are. The world needs more girls like you.*

*When Simon shares all later, I can't help but wish I had been there. To see the way you turned heads when you entered the restaurant, the jealous glances from other women who desire to be as beautiful as you, the sly eyes of men who want more. He says you were cheerful and unsuspecting, the way I like it. I'm so glad you are back into the fold again.*

**Abby - April 2018**

The shimmering lake catches my eye, sparkling like a million tiny diamonds dotted along the surface. It is a perfect day. The warm sun is beating down on our backs making it almost feel like spring. Harry tells me he loves me and I am in heaven. There is nothing more perfect than this. When I am with him the beauty of the surroundings suddenly stand up and say "aren't we beautiful?" and I wonder how I missed it all.

Then in one fell swoop my perfect life falls apart.

It is an innocent conversation that gets me wondering, well more of an argument between Mum and Dad. It's not unusual these days but something about the way Dad says 'I was busy doing work,' when Mum questions where he was, makes me stop and think. It isn't what he says it is the way he says it. He sounds insincere, like a lie he's told many times before.

Mum is complaining. 'I'm tired of being left here in limbo.'

'It'll be sorted soon'

He doesn't sound like he means that either. I start to wonder what exactly Dad does do for work. I should know but I've always switched off whenever he's mentioned it. Dad has always been a bit of an enigma to me, especially recently. One minute he is our loving Dad, full of hugs and laughs, acting like a little kid, the next minute he'll be grumpy and won't want to talk to anyone. I assumed everyone's dad were like that.

When I'm working it'll be different. I'll do a job I enjoy and I won't care about the money. I won't shout at my kids the whole time. I'll spend time with them.

I watch Dad from my window as he heads to the car to go out again for more "work" related activities.

'Mum, what does Dad actually do?' Mum is sitting by herself at the dining table, scrolling through endless posts on Facebook. She glances up with a surprised expression.

'What does he do?'

'I mean for work.'

'He runs his own business.'

'Yeah but what is his business?'

She seems unsure and I'm getting the feeling even she doesn't know. 'Something to do with property management. He doesn't talk about it much, it's boring apparently.'

I nod and leave, pondering what this means. I don't have a chance to think long before a text pings on my phone.

*Hey baby. Missed you. Fancy a walk in the woods?*

My heart jumps at the words from Harry. He misses me. I leap up, grab my coat.

'Where you going?' Beth is at my feet. She has sneaked up on me before I can even blink.

'You know where.' She turns her necklace over and back again. 'It'll be fine.'

'Be careful.'

'I will, I promise.'

Beth worries too much, and I understand why, but I'm not her and this is not the same situation.

I put Beth and Dad out of my mind as I practically skip down the hill. Harry is waiting at his usual spot, a big grin on his face.

'There she is, the most beautiful girl alive.'

I blush. No one has ever said that to me before. He pulls me in for a kiss. We walk and walk until Harry turns to me, eyes full of questions.

'Hey Abby, I was wondering,' he begins nervously, running his fingers through his hair. 'Do you want to … you know … get more intimate with me?' My mind is in turmoil, of course I do but I don't know if it's right. 'My Nan has a flat near here.' My eyes widen at what he is suggesting. Could I go along with a boy I've only just met to a strange place?

'Um maybe,' I reply because I don't want to come out and say it outright. His face falls.

'You don't want to? It's too soon?'

'It's just that- '

'I know. I know. We haven't known each other long, but I feel this connection between us. Don't you feel it?'

'Of course I do but- '

'No buts, if you want this we can do it. Forget your parents. They sound way too overprotective anyway.'

I rack my brains to think of what I'd said that made Mum and Dad sound too overprotective. I don't even remember mentioning them much at all. Suddenly this feels weird. I would be stupid to jump into anything after what happened to Beth.

'I can't today but I'll think about it.' I berate myself for being so wussy. Why can't I come and say no? Isn't that what they taught us in Sex Ed. Just say no. Except it's not easy in real life when you are staring into the face of perfection and you don't want to lose him.

'Tomorrow then?'

'Yeah, maybe.'

The mood is ruined for the rest of the afternoon. He is quiet. I have ruined it but I don't want to jump into bed with him, not yet. I leave him at the tree and wonder if I'll see him again.

## August 2017

*Simon tells me you are slipping away, that you seem distant. What's going on, love? Surely you don't want to break up with him? He's worried you are going to run away. Why would you do that? You need him. You're only a child, despite what you think. You're barely old enough to make your own decisions. Why can't you trust him? You argue with him, answer him back. Why, when you have something so beautiful, do you risk it all?*

*You fill me with rage. Simon says you want independence, and that you are fed up with being with men who try to control your life. Have you forgotten so quickly how tough it is on your own? I only want to look after you. Why can't you understand that? You are nothing on your own. You can't survive out there without someone taking care of you. There are others like Simon, don't think you can escape them.*

*Girls like you would be lost without me.*

*You let your anger get the better of you in your latest argument, you lost it and chucked a plant pot at the wall. You screamed at him and told him you didn't need him and that you wanted your life back. What life exactly? The life on the streets where you wondered where the next plate of food was coming from, or the life where you were so high on drugs you didn't know what day it was?*

*Wake up Beth, you can't do it alone.*

*I see you storm out of his apartment, defiant, shouting back at him. He loves you, why can't you see that? The problem with you is that you can't see that relationships take time and work, none of which you appear to want to do. You march away, clipping on your high heels. Who bought you those high heels? Don't you forget that.*

*Now I'm back to spying on you. I can't trust Simon to do a simple job. Where are you going, sweet love?*

*You stop when you reach the park and sit down on the bench, head in your lap. The older mothers in the corner crowd closer to their children, they see you as a threat but you notice none of that. Are you contemplating life? Where you went wrong? I will you to go back to him.*

*Eventually you stand up, seeming considerably calmer, and walk slowly back to his apartment. Your feet must hurt in those heels, adrenaline got you here but it's a hard slog back.*

*He greets you at the door, face full of sadness. You throw yourself into his arms. That's a good girl. I knew you'd do the right thing. He gently guides you back in, arm possessively round your waist. You made up that night didn't you? You can't resist the lure of a loving man. He would have told you what you so desperately wanted to hear and you would have smiled contentedly because that's where you want to be.*

*Don't leave him again. You need him. I can only keep you safe when you are with him.*

## Beth - May 2018

'What's up with you? You seem upset since you got back.'

'Do I?' Abby acts innocent but I can see it in her eyes. Something went on today. I need to find out what.

'Come on Abby, you can talk to me. I'm not going to judge.'

'He asked me to sleep with him, said he had a flat.' Inside I am horrified, the thought of history repeating itself, but outside I am as calm as I can be.

'And did you?'

'No,' she answers quickly, shocked that I would even suggest that. Phew. 'Of course not.'

'You did the right thing.'

'Did I? What if he dumps me? What if he hates me now? What if he thinks I'm frigid and never wants to see me again?'

'Then he's not worth it. Abby, you have just met the guy. He can't expect you to be jumping into bed with him however horny he is.'

'But what if he dumps me?' she cries.

I feel her pain, really I do, but I also don't want her to get hurt. Yeah it could be innocent and he just wants to sleep with her but to me he sounds like a creep taking advantage of a teenager. 'Besides it's against the law.'

'It is?'

'You're under sixteen. He could be prosecuted.'

She seems relieved that she has a good excuse to give. 'Oh.'

I want to tell her to ditch him right now but I can't do that. If I plunge in there heavy handed it'll just make her want to see him even more. Believe me, I know.

'Don't do anything you're not comfortable with. Don't let him force you.'

'You're right, thanks.' I realise that her and I aren't that different after all. She's me, seven years ago. For years I've wished I could turn back time and make different decisions. Now I can, sort of. I may not be able to change my actions but hopefully I can influence hers. I just need to figure out the best way to go about it.

I worry when she goes out again to meet him. Part of me is hoping he won't turn up. Cruel - in the short run but better off in the long run.

I follow her even though she makes me promise not to. I have to make sure she is safe. I position myself far enough not to be seen but close enough to make out what is going on.

I already hate his smarmy expression and the way he leans over, trying to possess her.

I will Abby to say no to him.

When his expression quickly turns to anger I know she has. He clutches his head, scrapping his fingers through his hair. It makes my blood boil. You're allowed to say no.

He looks like he has been punched in the stomach and is in severe pain.

Abby's head darts around, searching for help.

I move forward into ear shot. I'm glad I came. This is getting out of hand. He grabs her arm and starts to pull her towards the lake. His voice is deeper than I'd imagined. 'I am disappointed Abby. I was hoping our love meant more to you than that.' What a creep. 'Come with me. You won't be sorry.'

I am right behind them and he still hasn't spotted me.

'It does mean everything to me, and it doesn't mean I don't want to, just not now,' pleads Abby.

That's it. I can't hold back anymore. I rush forward and yell at the top of my voice. 'Let my sister go.' He turns, eyes wide, and sees me. Within seconds I am standing in front of them, Harry still gripping my sister's arm. 'Get your hands off her.' But Harry isn't giving up.

'You must be Beth.' A slow smile creeps across his face and a cold shiver runs down my spine. How does he know my name? 'Michael will be delighted to know you are here.'

Every muscle in my body is frozen to the spot and I can't speak. Abby tries to get away but Harry pulls her back. I grab at his arm but he is stronger than he seems. Harry's vicious punch catches me by surprise and I stumble backwards landing awkwardly on the gravel path.

'Don't you worry Beth, we'll be back for you.'

He pulls on Abby's arm and drags her away from me. I feel bruised and useless but more than that, I feel the anger building up inside me. I grab the closest thing, a sharp, fist sized rock. I'm on my feet and chasing after them before I know what I'm doing. Harry sees me and finally looks scared as I swing the rock at his head. He falls to the floor with a red gash on his head and finally Abby is free.

Using all the anger that's built up from the way I've been treated, I lift the rock above my head aiming it dead centre at Harry's cowering face.

'Beth?' Abby's voice snaps me out of my rage, and gives Harry the chance to scramble to his feet. 'You were right about him.'

'And your father was right about you,' Harry shouts as he sprints away.

I turn and stare at him. 'What did you say?'

## August 2017

*So you left then. What a silly girl. You need him. You'll soon see. Why can't you understand that I only want what's best for you? That's all I've ever wanted. Everything I have done is for you and our family. I set up this business for your Mum, and you, and then Abby. You had an amazing house, all the things you could ever want, but you chose to run away, destroying our marriage. Now you are running again. Oh dear daughter, when will you realise that this business has paid for our lives? You are threatening everything.*

*You see child, you had it easy when you were growing up, loving parents, all the attention. What did I have apart from misery, heartache and a father who hated me? I love you more than you will ever know but you don't appreciate that. This business is the only thing that made me feel good after what I went through back then. You have no idea what it was like: I was controlled. Now I'm the one in control. But I feel it slipping away from me. You are the threat that could undo all the good I've ever done.*

*Your Mum doesn't understand. All she thinks about is you.*

*We had a good marriage before.*

*It wasn't perfect, of course not, but we had everything until you had to go and ruin it by being a selfish teenager. And I'm stuck with a depressed wife and a whiny child. She's never got over you leaving. I fear she will never recover. You are a stranger to her now. You have seen things which she shouldn't know about. Stay with Simon, that's the best thing, then I'll know I have you under control.*

*I can't afford for you to go rogue.*

*Simon doesn't even know where you went. He woke up and found you were gone. If it were me I would not have let it happen. 'But you did,' I hear you say.*

*When you ran away with Michael, he took care of you, he was everything a man could wish for his daughter. But it was never good enough for you. Nothing I do is ever enough for anyone. I've spent my whole life trying to prove my worth but no one cares.*

*I thought I would feel powerful and invincible but it turns out you can't make people love you. I can't buy the love that is missing from my life. My mother never cared about me the way Emily cares about you. She would die for you. You only have to see the way you have torn apart her life .*

*Have you any idea how that makes me feel?*

## Abby - May 2018

'How does he know Michael?' I ask, running out of breath as we jog up the hill back towards the cottage. None of what we've heard is computing in my brain. 'And what did he mean about Dad?'

'I don't know. I'm thinking.' I'm definitely not cut out for hills as I try to keep up with the furious pace that she is going, stumbling over patches of grass.

Images of my loving father, hugging me, consoling me, flash before me. I am trying to override the feelings of dread that are threatening to take over my mind.

'The bastard! The absolute bastard!' Her face is going a darker shade of red with every word while marching ahead so fast that I am practically having to run behind her.

'Who, Michael?'

'Dad.'

'I don't understand. What's Dad done?'

'Oh my god, I can't deal with this,' she says, her anger turning to anguish. When we finally make it to the garden, She sits down on the picnic bench and puts her head in her lap. 'What are we going to do?' she wails, lifting her head. I drop down next to her, trying to catch my breath.

'Tell me what's going on?'

'Oh Abby, don't you get it? Dad is behind this.'

'Behind what?'

'He told Harry we're here. He knows Michael. What if Dad is running this whole thing?' Her words send vibrations of shock through my body as I struggle to understand what she is saying.

'You're trying to tell me that our Dad, a man we've known our whole lives, is somehow responsible for you going off with an older man, and now he is responsible for this.

She gives me a look, one I can't quite understand. I feel my face redden.

'Yes, Abby. Oh, you're so innocent. It makes sense now. Dad arranged this. He knew about this house. All the times when he was helping us. Don't you remember when he went out to find Michael but he had conveniently gone?'

'Maybe he had gone.'

'Abby, it is not a coincidence that you have met an older man hundreds of miles away from home. Dad is running some kind of prostitute business.'

'Don't be ridiculous! He's our Dad. He wouldn't do that.'

The more she speaks the more I feel confused but yet somehow it does seem clearer. The "business" he runs, none of us know what it really is; the lies he tells Mum, the amount of times he disappears off for work reasons.

'He wouldn't do that,' I repeat more for my benefit than anyone else. 'He wouldn't.'

'It looks like he has.'

We sit silently for a moment in our shock, staring at the mountains opposite us.

'Mum did say that he never seemed to help find you when you went missing seven years ago, that he didn't search properly.'

'She said that?'

'Not to me, but I heard her talking about it to Uncle Pete. He kept saying she should leave him. He has always seemed to hate him. I never understood why. She said she was always looking but he didn't seem to care.'

'Mum. We need to warn her!'

'What are we going to say?'

'That her husband of many years is a lying bastard.'

'What if he's there?' She considers for a moment.

'Then we wait and get Mum on her own. We can't let him know that we know.'

I am afraid. Who can tell what he is capable of? If he has lied to us for this long what else don't we know about him?

'I wish we could go home,' I say, whimpering like a little child.

She pulls me to her. 'It'll be okay. We will get away, don't you worry.'

I am not so confident but I want to believe her. My body, feeling heavy with the weight of the revelations, makes walking difficult, but I drag myself silently towards our cottage.

Mum and Dad are both out when we make it back. The quaint feel to the small house has taken a more sinister turn with the new knowledge. It doesn't feel safe anymore; It doesn't seem a place we can hide away in but a well-planned plot. He always meant to bring us here, to trap us in a secluded place. I despair at the fact that we trusted him so much, that even Detective Stevens - who knows nothing about where we are - thought he was taking us somewhere safe. How could we have got it so wrong?

We decide to hide out in our room, the furthest point from the front door. It feels the safest place, Beth sits down on my bed, her hands visibly shaking.

'Maybe we should phone the police?'

She nods. I reach for my phone but as usual for this stupid place it has no signal.

'Damn it.' Beth gets hers out but shakes her head.

Then we hear the key in the door.

## Beth - September 2017

I am free again. I left him, I left Simon. He was starting to control everything I did, like Michael. It feels as though a weight has been lifted from me. It was starting to be too familiar; the pretty dresses, the gifts, the meals out. I don't want that again. I didn't even tell him, sneaked out when he was asleep. He would have tried to persuade me to stay and I know what I'm like. A flash of his smile, a kind word and I would have stayed.

I have to be strong.

The only way I'm going to make it is if I go it alone. I don't need men and I certainly don't need those kinds of men.

I find myself walking the streets but I'm determined not to be homeless again. I will get my life together this time.

I have to survive.

I didn't escape everything to end up dead on the street. I still see Lily, her expression as she lay there after her overdose. She was lucky; she could have died.

I won't end up like that.

I walk down the high street, no plan, just survival on my mind. A job advert in a window catches my attention. 'Shop assistant wanted'. The shop is shut until morning but there is hope in those three words.

I make my way to the homeless shelter. It's dry at least, even if it is full of people I'd rather not hang around with. The woman at reception eyes me suspiciously.

'I need a place to stay,' I say, hoping she will understand without me having to go into too many details.

She thrusts a clipboard at me. 'Fill this out.'

'Thank you.' I quickly fill out the form; it's just for the night. Tomorrow I will change the world.

The shelter is noisy but it's warm and dry. Sleep is not something that will happen there. Men shout at each other until a woman shouts back at them: 'For goodness's sake, shut up the pair of you, some of us are trying to sleep.'

I must have slept as it is light out when I wake up. I jump out of bed. I need to get out of here.

I shout my thanks to the grumpy receptionist as I leave. She grunts something incoherent at me.

I have to get to the shop by the time it opens. I straighten down my dress. It'll do the job even though I have slept in it. They don't need to know that. I pull my fingers through my hair. I should have stopped to brush my hair properly. The shop assistant smiles at me as I enter.

'I'm here about the job,' I say pointing at the window.

'Oh … um I'm not sure it's still available.' Her words send me into despair. It must be. 'I'll check.' She leaves me alone while she goes out back. I rifle through the clothes. Whoa - these prices are crazy. Who can afford this stuff? They are nice though, stylish.

'You're in luck. The boss says the person they had lined up pulled out last night.'

'Yes!' I say with the enthusiasm of a child. She smiles.

'Do you have a CV?'

I didn't think of that.

'Um no. Sorry.'

'No worries. Come this way, the boss will see you now.'

I follow her. I'm expecting a posh older lady with high standards, I'm not prepared for an older, kind-faced man.

'I'm James.' He holds his hand out.

'Beth,' I answer, returning his handshake.

'So you don't have a CV and you've turned up a bit dishevelled.' I guess I'm not hiding it as well as I thought. I shrug, looking sheepish, feeling as if I am the biggest idiot ever. I'm about to walk out in shame when he adds 'So what's your story? Nice girl like you out on the street?'

I wonder how much I should tell him but his caring face makes me want to share everything. So I tell him, all the gory details and he doesn't throw me out. He smiles and tells me the job is mine. There is hope for me. For the first time ever I am making it on my own, the start of a journey.

Things can only get better now, can't they?

## Abby - May 2018

Beth and I sit frozen in her bed, holding on to each other, praying that Dad isn't back.

'Beth, Abby?' Mum's voice sounds outside our room. A huge sigh of relief escapes from me.

'In here,' I call. She opens the door, staring at us strangely, no doubt wondering why we are huddled together. 'Where's Dad?' I ask.

'Not home yet. What's going on?' I glance at Beth, uncertain of whether we should tell Mum, destroying the fantasy that she has.

'You can tell me,' Mum says, appearing to sound confident but I detect a hint of fear in her tone.

'We think we're in danger.' Beth tells her. 'And we think Dad's involved.'

'What?' Mum's eyes widen as she grabs her chest. I hate seeing her like that. I hate the fact that we are about to ruin her life. 'How do you know?'

I tell her about Harry and how close I came to being taken away, being drawn into his world.

Mum starts shaking, crying, she can't stop. 'I'm sorry, I'm so sorry. This is all my fault,' she manages finally.

'Why are *you* sorry?' Beth asks.

'I have failed to protect the only two people who really matter in my life. How could I have been so stupid.'

'Did you know?' I stare at Beth with confusion. Of course she didn't know, how could she?

'About your father?'

'Yes.'

'No, of course not but somehow it makes sense.' Beth nods. I can tell she feels the same.

'I found a letter,' I blurt out suddenly. Beth looks at me strangely. 'It was addressed to Freddie.' I search for a flicker of recognition from Mum but nothing.

'Who's Freddie?' she asks.

'It's from a counsellor asking how he is. It had our

address on it.'

'That doesn't make sense,' Mum replies, more confused than ever. She sits down on the bed.

'Mum, you need to get it together. We have to do something.' Beth, the first born daughter, is the one in control now. Mum looks deflated as if the life has been sucked out of her.

'Where's the letter?' she asks quickly. I take her to it. She immediately dials the number at the top of it.

'This is Emily,' she says, expecting that the other person will instantly know who she is. 'We received this letter addressed to Freddie. Who is he?' I can't hear the response on the other side but I can sense Mum's growing frustration. 'I understand that but our lives could be in danger … oh fine, yes … I'll have Freddie call you if ever I find out who he is.'

'You think Freddie is Dad, don't you?' asks Beth. Mum nods.

'We need to get out of here.' She is starting to sound desperate.

She is right, but I suddenly can't think. Where would we go? Do we have any money? Before I can consider it any further, the key is in the door. He is home. We stare at each other. Mum wipes away her tears quickly.

'Stay calm,' says Beth. 'Don't give anything away.'

But any pretence is shattered when I see his face. He has a look unlike any I have ever known on him. A look of pure evil.

He shakes his head. 'What am I going to do with you three?'

Beth appears as terrified as I feel.

'Why couldn't you just go with Harry?' His eyes pointing directly at me and I think I will start crying but I don't.

Beth stands up in defiance. 'You can't hurt us anymore.'

Dad lets out a horrible, heartless laugh. 'You think you

can outwit me? I've been outsmarting all of you for decades.'

I can bear it no longer. 'How could you?' I lunge at him and push him into the wall. 'We are your children,' I scream at him. 'This is your wife.' I keep pushing him, the rage and excess tension pouring out of me. He stands there, face calm and smug, satisfied there is nothing I can do.

'Oh Abby, you always were so naïve.' It's only after the slap on his face that he gets angry. 'I suggest you stop before someone gets really hurt.' He throws me onto my bed. Mum and Beth watch horrified. Beth strokes my head. I should be comforting her. Mum is still sitting there, staring at Dad, frozen, as if she is numb from shock.

'You stupid girls.' He leaves, shutting the door behind him. I am relieved there is no lock but am wondering what he is planning now. I put my head on the bed in despair.

'Don't worry, we'll get out of here,' says Beth. I forget she has done this before.

'Can't we walk out?' I ask.

'What if he's waiting there?' Mum's voice almost sounds like a child.

'He's probably panicking. We know his big secret. He doesn't have a plan right now. I'll bet he's pacing around trying to figure out what the hell to do.' She's right.

'We have to figure out a strategy first,' I say, finally feeling like I'm getting it together.

'Exactly.' Mum looks at us both, unsure but trusting. Beth walks over to the window. I wonder if she is considering jumping out of it and figuring out whether we could survive that big a jump. 'Do you have your phone, Abby?'

A silly question, I always have my phone on me. I pull it out. 'No signal.' I wave it about. 'Who would I text anyway?' Then Mum remembers something.

'This is who,' she says, pointing at a number on a piece of paper. Next to it is written the name of a detective.

Amazingly, Mum's phone has a signal. We urge her on as she types a message.

*This is Emily Kimmings in the Lake District. We are at Apple Tree Cottages, Keswick. We are in danger. Jack is the one behind this whole thing.*

She sends it excitedly. They will come, I know they will. I watch as the message says sending. It takes a long time. *Failed to send. Retry.* Damn. She clicks on retry but it doesn't work.

'Don't panic Mum,' Beth says calmly and I wonder how she can be so calm.

'Dial 999 as well,' suggests Mum.

'We have no signal,' I repeat.

'It doesn't matter. It'll work.'

But before I can make the call, the door opens. I grab the phone and hide it under Beth's pillow. Dad stands before us, so sure of himself, holding a gun. My blood runs cold.

'Right girls, we are going on a trip.' None of us move. 'That means get up and get in the car,' he demands impatiently, waving his gun towards the door. We stand up and follow. I carefully slide the phone from under the pillow into my pocket, it now says "sent".

I have to hope that any help that comes will be able to find us.

**Beth - September 2017**

'My name is Beth and I'm a drug addict.' I take a deep breath and wish I could disappear into the floor below me. I've finally said it and no one is judging me. The circle of people around me smile and nod.

'Welcome Beth,' exclaims Natalie, the organiser, loudly. 'Why don't you tell us your story?'

'It's pretty long,' I say quietly.

She beams kindly, 'We have time.'

'I was an idiot.' No one shouts out that I wasn't. 'When

I was fifteen, I met an older man who I believed loved me. He persuaded me to move out of home and in with him. He made me feel special.' I see a few nods from the older women. A couple of the men shuffle in their seats uncomfortably

'To start with he was so kind, not forcing me to do anything I didn't want to do. He bought me gifts and pretty dresses and took me to posh restaurants. I felt so special. Man, I was so naïve.'

An older lady chips in. 'It's alright dear, we all have our stories. None of us are perfect but this sounds very much like he was taking advantage of you.'

'He was, but I didn't realise it. He came home one day upset, saying he'd got involved with the wrong people and he needed my help. My help was going on a date with another man. What I thought was another date turned into sex.'

The older lady's mouth falls open and her eyes narrow.

'I've been trying to make it on my own but it's so hard.' I am openly sobbing now, any pride I had has gone out of the window.

The lady reaches over and puts her arm around me. 'It's okay,' she says comfortingly and everyone else nods or murmurs their agreement.

'Please help me,' I whisper quietly.

'Of course we will,' reassures Natalie. 'We are here for you.'

'We totally are,' nods the older lady in agreement.

Natalie turns to her. 'Delores, why don't you tell us how your week has been?'

I am grateful for the break as Delores, the older lady, begins her story, still holding on to me.

'I've had a great week surprisingly. I saw my granddaughter for the first time in a year.'

'Oh, wow. Your daughter finally agreed to meet up?' asks Natalie.

'Yes, and it was wonderful. Of course she was wary but

she could see that I've changed.' She turns to me. 'I was a mess two years ago when I joined this group, a big fat alcoholic mess.' She laughs, I smile. I can't imagine this strong woman being any different to the way she is. It gives me hope.

One day I will be that strong too.

**Abby - May 2018**

We follow Dad to his car, unable to speak, scared. I can't stop staring at the gun in Dad's hand. Would he really use it on his own family?

I am freezing despite wearing a thick jumper. The spring like weather should warm me up but I can't stop shaking. The shock of finding out that my own father is responsible for this turmoil in our lives is hard to digest.

I hold onto Beth's hand and she shoots me a reassuring smile. I am sure she is already planning our escape, any moment now she will divert us to Mum's car. There is no way we can get into his car with him. We have to find a way out of this. I am forced to let go of her hand as we squeeze out of the narrow front door.

Outside is desolate, no one around, not even an animal. The sight of Dad's car, shiny, flashy, brings new meaning now. All the times that I've happily enjoyed the luxury of it, marvelled at the gadgets, revelled in the heated seats, and it was all lies. A car bought with lies.

Barf Mountain looms over us, taunting us with memories of happier times. All lies. The path we walked along, laughing and joking. All lies.

Dad unlocks the car with his remote. He holds the back door open for me and I consider how much it would take to overpower him. He seems stronger now than ever before, a monster who has suddenly doubled in size. When I don't move he gets impatient.

'Get in Abby. I don't have time for this.'

He shoves me in roughly, taking me by surprise, before

I can resist. This is not the loving father I have grown up with. I turn around with the intention of getting out again but the door is already shut and locked. I am waiting for Beth and Mum to get in but he gets in the driver's seat and locks the door. He's only taking me!

The panic in Beth's eyes, the frantic tugging of the locked door handle, the banging on his window - none of it makes any difference. Mum stands frozen to the spot, horrified yet unable to spring to action. I pull the door lever in a pointless attempt to get out. I know it will make no difference.

To my horror, Dad starts driving and I can only stare at the faces of my sister and Mum, not dreaming for one moment that I would be kidnapped by my own father. My breathing speeds up. I need to get out. I can't breathe. I need to escape. I can't breathe.

Get it together.

I have to survive.

I clutch the side of the car and try to block out the images put in my head by Beth. Images of when she was kidnapped; men leering at her in expensive restaurants, being trapped in a bedroom with different men. Is this going to be my fate?

You can do this. You will survive.

'Where are we going?' I finally manage to stutter. He ignores me, staring straight ahead. Who is this stranger?

'Dad, please, let me go.' I have to appeal to his fatherly side. He wouldn't abandon me to it, would he? 'Dad, I want to go home?'

He laughs cruelly. 'You think you have a home now?' His voice is cold, unkind, not like my Dad.

'How can you do this to your own daughter? Your youngest daughter.' I say youngest thinking it makes me somehow special but it's clutching at straws really.

He merely sniggers. 'You know nothing child.'

And I am beginning to realise he is right. I am naïve. Beth tried to warn me. I should have told Harry where to go when I first met him. How could I have ever believed that such a boy would actually want me? I kick myself for being so stupid, for not following the advice of my own sister. The sister who has been through this.

Why did I think I was so special that it wouldn't happen to me?

'Don't worry darling. They'll take care of you.'

'Who?' But I already know who: the men.

'I've got lots of friends who will take care of you.'

I'm struggling to understand how he can have men here and back at home. What kind of business is he running? How can he do it all? I hope Beth has a plan or I'm screwed.

'Dad, who's Freddie?' I ask suddenly. He doesn't answer straight away and I see his eyes in the mirror, a small lost boy.

'Just someone I knew,' he answers finally.

**Beth - November 2017**

'Two months and clean,' I announce proudly. The familiar faces in the circle smile encouragingly.

'And how are you feeling in yourself?' asks Jimmy.

'Great. I'm healthy, I'm happy but- ,'

'But what?'

'I keep thinking about my parents.'

'What about them?'

'I saw a show the other day, Long Lost Family.'

'I love that show,' shouts Gemma, blushing slightly when everyone stares at her. 'Sorry.'

'Carry on.' Jimmy urges me on with a grin.

'And there was this Mum who had given up her daughter for adoption and then they got together and she was so happy. They were hugging and crying.' Gemma's eyes well up. 'And I thought what if my Mum was that happy when I go back.'

'You don't think she will be?'

'I'm afraid. What if she doesn't want to see me? What if she's forgotten me and moved on?'

'Do you really think your own mother wouldn't be happy to see you?' asks Delores. 'If you were my daughter, I'd be tearing my hair out not being with you.'

'You actually think she'd feel that way?'

'Yes,' shouts the group in unison.

'Go see her,' says Delores.

'I don't know.'

~

I lay in bed that night, the different scenarios running through my head. I return, they are happy, they hug me, life goes back to normal - is that possible?

I return, they reject me, tell me to go away again - is that likely?

I return, they don't recognise me or worse they've moved and I can't even find them, or maybe they've divorced and the family is fragmented.

My mind is exploding with all the possibilities. What is the worst thing that could happen if I went back? What would be the best thing? I picture Mum hugging me, so happy to see me but Dad is standing back, not willing to accept that I am there.

Do it or not do it?

How can I even begin to explain what happened with Michael?

I can still hear Delores' voice echoing in my head. 'Just go back.'

She's right. Mum would be happy. Of course she would. Why wouldn't she be? She gave birth to me.

*I'm doing it.* I don't expect a response to the text message I've sent Delores in the middle of the night but she instantly replies.

*You go girl.* I can feel her energy transferring to me.

~

It's almost Christmas when Delores turns up at my door.

'Seriously girl, why are you still here?'

'I can't do it.'

'Yes, you can. Go there. What's the worst thing that can happen?'

I don't want to list all the horrible realities that have been running through my head. She hovers at the door, shuffling from one foot to the other to keep warm.

'Do I have to drag you there?'

'No,' I laugh. 'I'll go tomorrow.'

'Great idea, Christmas Eve. They'll be so happy to see you. And if you don't I'll kick your arse.'

'I can always rely on you to spur me into action.'

I pack my bag and climb into bed for the last time. I'm really doing this.

~

The morning finally dawns and I am up and dressed early.

I am shaking throughout the bus journey. Several times I almost go back, but Delores' voice keeps me going. I'm finally going to see my parents.

**Beth - May 2018**

We watch helplessly as the man I thought was my loving father for more than twenty years drives away with my little sister. This can't be happening. I can't move, I screamed and banged on the car but it did no good. I tried but I couldn't help her. Mum is standing next to me shaking, staring into space.

'Mum, Mum, get a grip!' I say, grabbing her arm.

A sense of rage fills her. 'He is not going to do this again,' she shouts.

Fully awakened from her trance, she pulls her car keys out of her pocket.

'Get in,' she shouts, pushing me towards her car. Dad's car has disappeared from view.

'Text the detective again.' She throws her phone at me as I climb in the front seat next to her.

We drive round the next corner and see them. My sister

is in sight. Mum's face is set in stone, concentrated on her goal of getting her daughter back.

I glance over at her uneasily, it feels like an evil force has taken over her body.

Maybe it has.

'Mum?'

'Yes?'

'Did you ever think about divorcing Dad when I was away? You hear of couples falling apart when their child goes missing.'

'The morning of the day you returned we had a big row and he said he wanted a divorce.'

'A divorce?'

'Then you came back.'

'You stayed together for me?'

'Yes we did. Probably a mistake. I should have ditched him then. If I'd known I would have taken you and Abby somewhere far away, somewhere safe.'

'How could you have known about any of this? There's no way.'

'No, you're right. I didn't imagine for a minute that he was running a grooming business that entrapped you.'

'Crazy.' I shake my head.

'Did you love him?' she asks cautiously.

'Who?'

'Michael.'

'Yes I did. I thought he did too. How stupid was I?'

'Not stupid. We were both taken in.'

The speed we are doing means we reach his car quickly. I wonder what Mum is planning; drive alongside the car before leaping movie-style to his car? Does that work in real life? No, far too dangerous. Or she could ram him forcing him to slow down or stop. No - we might hurt Abby. I guess we have to play it safe and follow him. He wouldn't do anything stupid but that Dad is the old Dad; the new one is unpredictable, unknown.

'I'm sorry Mum,' I say quietly. She throws me a quick

look of confusion.

'Why?'

'This is all my fault.'

'How is it?'

'If I hadn't got involved with Michael in the first place, if I had stopped Abby meeting Harry- '

'Stop Beth. None of this is your fault. You were groomed by a man working for your father. You were fifteen. If it's anyone's fault it's mine, for not realising I was married to a sick bastard.'

I smile at this, her using a swear word.

'Don't worry honey, we'll get through this. He won't win. How are you getting on with that text?'

'No signal.' I wave it around hopefully. 'Oh wait. I think it's working. Message sent.'

'Great, well done.'

Out of the back of Dad's car we see Abby turn around with anxious eyes, begging us to save her.

And then Dad's car stops suddenly. Having no time to respond, Mum ploughs us into the back of Dad's car with full force. Glass smashing, metal crunching, the lights fades as I drift into unconsciousness. I have to stay awake. I have to save her.

~

'Mum, Mum.' I frantically shake her. She has to wake up. The road is a mess, glass everywhere, and so many bits of car that it's hard to tell which belongs to which. I hear sirens and pray that Abby is okay. I reach up and touch my forehead - wet, blood. But I'm alive.

It happened so quickly. I remember Dad's car stopping, me screaming, Mum screaming, then silence. We were thrown all over the place like a fairground ride. We spun, I'm sure we spun. I always hated spinny rides. I feel dizzy.

'Mum, wake up.' She groans. 'That's it, Mum. Open your eyes.' I've watched enough of Casualty to know that you have to keep them talking. 'Mum can you hear me?' You have to shout at them.

'Abby,' she mumbles.

'She'll be fine,' I say, even though I have no idea if that's true. Fear threatens to engulf me. I have to hold it together. I can fall apart later.

I undo my seat belt and shift a bit in my seat. My leg hurts but I can see no bones sticking out. That's got to be good, right?

I position myself towards Mum and lean into her face. Her breath on my face reassures me.

'Mum, stay with me.' Her eyes flicker, she is struggling to stay awake. 'Squeeze my hand,'

I force my hand into hers. I don't look at her injuries. I can't deal with that right now.

'The ambulance is on its way.'

The sirens grow louder as help draws closer. Flashing blue lights blind me. An angel comes to save me.

'Hey there, I'm Dave. I'm a paramedic. Don't move.' A mop of curly hair towers above me. Maybe not an angel but the friendliest looking man I have seen in months.

'Deal with Mum first,' I say. He nods and rattles off lots of words that I don't understand. I lay my head back, happy to let someone else take responsibility.

'What happened?'

'I don't know. They stopped suddenly. My sister is in the car in front, is she alright?'

'They'll be dealing with her right now. Don't worry about it.' But I am worried.

'With my Dad, he kidnapped her,' I add. 'Make sure they're not hurt.' He gives me a strange look but nods. Another paramedic appears at the driver door, their conversation is a jumble of medical terms that I can't concentrate on. Floppy haired Dave smiles at me reassuringly.

'We'll have you both out of here soon.'

Mum has to make it. I watch as they gently manoeuvre her onto a stretcher.

'Can I come too?' I ask, beginning to move.

'Wait there. We need to check you over first.' They carry her off. I'm not sure I can stand. I don't know if I'm injured or in shock.

'I'm fine,' I say to no one, feeling suddenly dizzy. 'Just save them.'

I close my eyes and let the world drift over me as everything goes black.

## Abby - June 2018

White walls, intense heat, whirring machines. I attempt to sit up. Where am I?

'Don't try to move. You're in hospital.' A man in blue hovers over me smiling softly. 'My name is Pete. I'm a nurse, and I'm going to be looking after you.'

'Mum?' I whisper.

'Your Mum is fine, so is your Dad.' Dad. For a moment I struggle to remember why I don't care that he is fine. Then everything he has done comes flooding back, filling me with rage once more. 'Where's Beth?'

The nurse doesn't say anything and tries to avoid my gaze.

'Where is she?' I demand.

'I'm so sorry but Beth didn't make it.'

'What?' I scream. 'She was fine. I saw her talking to Mum after we'd crashed. She can't be dead.'

'I'm sorry. She had a head injury. She was dead before they even got her to the ambulance.'

Tears stream down my face. My beautiful sister, dead.

'No, you're lying,' I say rudely. The nurse merely pats me on the arm. 'Tell me she's alive,' I scream.

'I'm sorry.'

My Beth is gone. I stare at the window barely comprehending this thought. Surely she's not dead. Then anger. 'I'm gonna kill him,' I growl.

The nurse pulls a confused face. 'Who honey?'

'Dad. He did this.'

'It was an accident. It's no one's fault.'

An accident of his making. He took Beth away from me and for that I will never forgive him. I can't even begin to explain this to the poor nurse who has no idea of the evil contained in my Dad.

'You can go and see your Mum and Dad soon if you like.'

'I never want to see him again,' I spit out venomously.

He pats my arm once more. 'You'll get through this.' I can't imagine anything being further from the truth. 'I'll get you some food.' He starts to walk away.

'Has a detective been in to see Mum?'

The nurse shakes his head. 'Not that I know of.'

I sent a text, I'm sure I did. My brain is so fuzzy I can't think straight. Where is the detective? I need to find Mum and get out of here. I have to find her. I try to move but I am connected to all these machines. I hadn't noticed the beeping noises they make before now as I sit up.

'Whoa, whoa, you can't get up. Sit down.' Alarmed, the nurse pushes me gently back down.

'I have to go. I have to get Mum.'

'Don't worry, she's fine. You're in shock, you need to rest.'

'I can rest later.' I try to resist but I am just too tired. My body feels like a ton of bricks.

'Lie back and relax. Food is coming in a minute.' Maybe he's in on it as well. What if he works for Dad? This whole thing has made me paranoid. I can't trust anyone. I close my eyes, defeated, helpless. I will find a way out of here.

~

When I wake up it is to the sound of a tray of food being placed on the table next to me. I am surprised to find I am hungry. The pie and chips look strangely appetising. I realise I haven't eaten in hours, maybe days. What day even is it?

The food makes me feel better instantly. Now is the

time. I pull the tubes out of me. Ouch that was worse than pulling off a plaster. I sit up, less dizzy than before, more stable. I can do this.

I make it to the end of the ward before I stumble and nausea overtakes me, but I have to keep going. Fortunately the nurses are otherwise occupied. They really should keep a better eye on their patients.

Then I see her, asleep and peaceful, alive and safe. I stagger over. I plant myself in the chair next to her and stroke her hair, to prove that she's really here. Then I remember that Beth isn't. Tears escape before I can swipe them away. Her eyes open. She can't see me crying. She smiles at the sight of me. 'Hey. How are you?' I ask, stupid question. She's not exactly great being in here.

'I'm okay.' But then her expression clouds over. She's remembered that Beth is dead. She reaches for my hand. I grab it a bit too forcefully, but it's so good to hold her again. Her hand is soft and warm. I wonder what Beth's hand is like, cold; I throw the thought out of my mind. I can't cope with that right now.

'The nurse told me about Beth.'

She turns away, trying to hide the tears I know are falling. I squeeze her hand tightly but this only seems to make the tears flow faster.

'I couldn't save her,' she whispers.

'What happened? I saw her alive in the car after we'd crashed.'

'I don't know. She was fine, then she wasn't. It should have been me.'

'No Mum, don't say that.' I'm sobbing now. I wonder if she would prefer to have me here or Beth. Another thought I can't deal with right now.

'Where's Dad?'

She shrugs. 'I don't know, but I hear he's fine,' she says angrily.

We sit in silence. I stroke her hand continuously and vigorously until I worry that I'm hurting her. 'Mum, we'll make it. Don't worry.' She smiles gently at me. I have no idea how we're going to make it but for now we both need to pretend.

~

The next morning a police officer arrives with the nurse.

'They want to talk to you about the accident.'

I nod as the man sits down in the chair next to me.

As I explain, I realise it sounds so far-fetched. Who would believe that my Dad is a criminal master-mind? He busily writes it down without a comment.

'So what's going to happen to Dad?'

'We'll speak to him.' His voice kind, but somewhat patronising.

When he is gone I beg them to move me next to Mum. I hate the idea of being alone right now. I am afraid. What if Dad comes after me?

The nurses say they have no room to move us. They seem confused about Dad. They act like I'm crazy. Next they'll be sending down a psychiatrist to check me out. I barely made it out of that car alive, Beth is dead. Surely they realise this is not an accident. I keep telling them he's responsible.

'Where's Dad?' I ask the nurse when she arrives the next morning to do my checks.

'He's a few wards away. He's fine. You must be worried about him.'

I should be and I guess I am. I also hate him but I have to see him.

'Can I talk to him?'

'Of course. I'll get the porter to wheel you over there this morning.'

So I wait. I wait for the moment when I can finally see the traitor of a messed up Dad who let me down in such a humongous way. Where do I even start in knowing what to say to him? I don't tell Mum when she visits. She would only get upset.

It's almost lunchtime by the time Mum has gone and I

finally get my chance. The porter is an old chirpy man with grey hair and a wispy beard. His cheerful chattering fills my head but I don't hear what he is saying. I only nod politely.

Dad is on his phone when we turn the corner into his ward. He doesn't even seem fazed by any of it. He's in hospital, on his phone, like nothing has happened, probably organising where his next girl is coming from. I want to punch him right then and there and keep punching him until he suffers what I feel right now.

When he sees me his face broadens into a huge smile, no remorse or anything.

I am not fooled.

He waves slightly before putting down his phone. The porter positions me next to his bed and says something about coming back in a little while.

'Hi Abby,' he says slowly. I don't reply. I don't know how to say all the things that are going on in my head. 'So good to see you. Glad that you didn't get hurt from the accident.'

I wonder if I imagined the whole thing. Did this same loving father actually kidnap me?

'She's dead you know,' I say finally. The colour drains from his face.

'Mum?' The expression of horror on his face says it all.

'No, Beth.' His face changes. I can't read it. 'You killed her.'

'Abby … I-'

'Abby what? Sorry? Really?'

He opens his mouth but shuts it again.

'See, you're not even sorry. You're a murderer.' I am shouting now but I don't care. 'You don't even care that you killed your daughter.' I grab hold of his arm.

'What is wrong with you?' For once he looks sad. Sad that his daughter is dead or sad that a girl who made him money is dead? I tighten my grip in anger. He doesn't stop me.

A nurse is by my side, grabbing me. 'Love stop. You'll

hurt him.'

'I want to hurt him,' I sob, tears furiously running down my face. 'I want to kill him. Why did you do it?' I ask him but he doesn't reply. Maybe even he doesn't know.

The nurse doesn't understand, no one does.

'He's a paedophile,' I shout. Dad glances around frantically. I can already see the faces of those around us turning to support me. I'm not sure that is the right label for him but I can't think what else to call him. It was the first thing I thought of. 'You don't know what he's done. Call the police.'

'Wait honey. I think you've got a bit mixed up. She's had a very traumatic day,' he tells the nurse.

'Don't you dare turn this on me,' I yell. 'You were going to kidnap me.' The old lady next to us turns pale.

'Porter, let's get Abby back.' The porter appears out of nowhere, he must have been waiting for me.

'Come on, dear, let's go.' He wheels me away. I glance one last time at Dad who is showing no real sorrow, no shame at what he's done. I don't feel I've ever known him. The times I cuddled him in bed, lay my head on his chest while he read me a book, all lies. The man I knew as my father was not a real person.

Mum is waiting by my bed when I get there. 'What's up? Where have you been?'

'I went to see him. He's not even sorry. Beth's dead and he doesn't even care,' I sob.

'Oh darling.' She pulls me close to her and I am grateful to have one parent that still loves me at least.

'Have you seen him yet?' Darkness fills Mum's eyes.

'Yes, I saw him this morning.'

'What did you say?'

'I can't repeat the words I said to him, they are not suitable for someone your age but lets just say he understands exactly how I feel about him.' I smile. 'Hopefully the police will sort him out.'

'I told the policeman who came to see me this morning but he didn't seem to believe me.'

'Yeah I saw him too. I don't think he understood.'

'We have to call that detective,' I say firmly sitting up.

'Yes, do it.' She pulls out her phone and starts dialling. I don't hear what she says as she walks away. I strain to listen but it's too noisy in here. I lay my head back on the pillow and wish that my life were different. I wish Beth was still alive and that Dad was not. At least when Beth was missing, Dad was Dad and Mum was happy. But was she happy? I wonder if she's ever been, not since Beth went away. She's always had a gaping hole in her, and now that hole will never be filled.

'What did she say?'

'No answer.'

'Could you not speak to someone else?'

'It's her mobile. I left a message. We'll sort this out, don't worry.'

But I do worry. I worry that he will come after us. That this life will never be normal again. I can't even remember what normal is anymore. Did I ever know normal?

Later on I sneak down there to see Dad. I'm not sure what my intentions are. He's asleep, so peaceful. Lucky him being able to sleep when my sister is dead. I sit down beside him. I could pull out the wires around him, smother him with a pillow. No one is here to stop me. Before I can explore these thoughts anymore he wakes up and looks up at me. There is something in his eyes I don't recognise, fear, and a sense that he is lost.

'I'm sorry Abby,' he begins. I put my hand up to stop him.

'Sorry is not good enough.'

'You don't understand.'

'What is there to understand? You kidnap girls and sell them to men.'

He sighs. 'I'm Freddie.' His words throw me. What does he mean? I don't understand. 'My name isn't Jack.'

'You've got a different name, so what?'

'Freddie was who I was, who I used to be.'

'Why did you change your name?' As much it pains me to have a civilised conversation with him, I want to find out what's going on.

'Freddie was abused as a child by his father. Freddie had an older brother who died tragically, that's when it started to go wrong for him.' The way he is talking about himself in the third person is creeping me out. 'Freddie always felt powerless, out of control.' His scared, childlike expression changes into one more stern. 'I vowed I would never feel that powerless again.'

I stand up, feeling as if I'm talking to a stranger, one who is scaring me. I realise I've never known my father.

~

'You're going home today,' declares the nurse cheerfully.

'Home?' I say confused. I'm not even sure where that is anymore.

'Yes they're ready to let you and your Mum and Dad go back to your cottage.'

'I'm not going back there,' I say firmly, and certainly not with him. But where else can I go? The nurse scurries off before I can discuss it further.

Panic engulfs me at the thought of being trapped back in that house with Dad. Mum appears at the door.

'Did they tell you we're going home?' I ask her.

'Yes but don't worry there is no way we're going back there.'

I sigh with relief. 'Have you tried the detective again?'

'I did but no answer.'

'Why wouldn't she answer?'

She shrugs. 'I was about to try the station.'

'Go ahead. You can do it here.' Her eyes dart around maybe wondering if someone will stop her.

She climbs into the bed next to me. I snuggle up to her

as she dials the number. She puts it on speaker phone so I can hear everything.

'Can I speak to Detective Stevens?'

'I'm sorry. She doesn't work here anymore.'

'What? Are you serious?'

'Yes is there anyone else that could help?'

'She was working on our case.'

'I'll put you through to Detective Johnson, he can advise you.'

Detective Johnson sounds like he has one too many things on his mind and a crazy middle-aged woman is not what he needs. When Mum explains the case to him all she gets is silence. I wonder at one point if he has hung up but he murmurs a little as if to reassure her. When she has finished we are both waiting for him to tell us who is working on it now but instead he has a disappointing response.

'I'm sorry Mrs Kimmings, there doesn't seem to be any record of this case.'

'What? There must be. Please check again. Our lives are in danger. My eldest daughter is already dead.'

'I tell you what I'll do, I'll go through the files again to make sure and I'll get back to you.' I've heard that one before. He is clearly fobbing her off so he can get on with something else.

'Detective Johnson, you don't understand, we have nowhere to live. We are being discharged from hospital today and they are expecting us to go back to the holiday cottage.'

'I'm sorry, I'm confused. Why can't you go home?'

She sighs.

'Because there are men from my husband's business chasing us. They will take my other daughter.'

'Right.'

I want to scream in frustration at him down the phone but that will get us nowhere.

'Please,' she whispers.

'Mrs Kimmings, I'll do my best. I'll call you back soon.'

He hangs up before she can argue with him. It seems we are all alone in the world with no one to help us. Even the police have given up on us. One thing is for sure, we are not going back to that cottage.

When the nurse arrives to check on me it's a different one, a woman this time.

'Where's the other nurse?' I ask.

'He's gone off shift. You've got me now. I'm Katie.' She has a bright smile and blonde hair to match. I trust her; she will help us. As I explain it to her she looks suitably shocked in the right places.

'We want to go to a women's refuge,' Mum explains. Why hadn't I thought of that?

'Of course, you can't go back there.'

'But please don't tell my husband.'

'I'll find out the details of one. Don't worry.'

She is back by our side within thirty minutes armed with information about the local women's refuge.

'They are expecting you later today. The doctor will be round in about an hour to sign the discharge papers for you both.'

'Thank you so much,' Mum says, putting her hand on the nurse's arm. She smiles softly and I wish that she would always take care of us.

~

*Moving On* is in a smart-looking house. There are no signs on the outside of the building so that women are safe, away from their violent husbands. The leaflet is full of kind faces and well-kept bedrooms. I am reassured just flicking through it.

When we arrive we are greeted by Sheena. I wonder if that is her real name. I also wonder if she once was a victim of domestic violence. I don't feel that we are in the same category as the others. Dad was never violent. We never felt we were in danger, We are the fools who were completely taken in by the man we loved, not even suspecting him for one minute, risking our lives.

I expect *Moving On* to be a sad place full of sad people with forlorn memories but nothing could be further from the truth. The vibrant colours instantly hit me when we walk in. The cheesy quotes, such as 'Don't give up, it's not over yet' on the walls make me smile. Everyone we meet welcomes us with a broad smile. We have gained a new family. Mum starts crying. I stare at her strangely.

'We're safe now Mum.'

'I'm not sad. It's just everyone is so nice. I didn't expect it.'

'Often it's after the stress that people's emotions take over,' says Sheena wisely 'We're through here, about to eat dinner.'

It's great here, but I know we can't stay forever.

~

I never thought a women's refuge would be fun. There are even other girls my age and some a few years older who have escaped abusive boyfriends. We pop into each other's bedrooms for a chat and share our stories as if we are on a school trip. I know Mum doesn't want to talk but all I can do is talk. It's my therapy. Whenever I think of Beth my heart wants to break. I still can't believe she is gone. If I let it, the sadness would weigh me down but I can't afford for that to happen. I have to be strong.

I would love to stay here forever. At night I lay in bed and dream of us growing old in this place, having kids and sharing our meals together. But I know that it won't always be like this. One day it will end.

It is that end that terrifies me.

I am safely cocooned in this bubble but one day I will be plunged into the real world again. Then what will I do? How do you just move on from what happened?

According to my counsellor everything I feel is normal. I'm pretty sure she says that to everyone who comes in here. Despite that, I like her. She is kind and doesn't judge me. She doesn't blame me for what happened even though

I do. In fact, she is outraged when I do blame myself.

'How could it be your fault?' she exclaims. But somehow it is. I met Harry and that led to Beth's death. It is my fault she is dead. I know logically that doesn't make sense but I can't get over feeling that it's true.

Mum is still sad. I hate seeing her like this. She mopes around reading books and I know she wants to cry but doesn't because she's trying to be brave for me. I give her a hug and hope that's enough.

We are into our second week at the refuge when the unthinkable happens.

'He's here,' whispers Mum furiously at me.

'Who?' But I know and the sound of the door buzzer going off repeatedly terrifies me.

'Dad. He's outside the gate.' I peer out of the window and see Dad pacing angrily while stabbing the buzzer without stopping.

'Bloody answer the door,' he's saying.

'What are we going to do?' I ask, clutching Mum's arm.

'Don't worry, I'll deal with this.' Sheena swoops in and picks up the telecom phone.

'How can I help you?' she asks in a very call centre voice. She's obviously done this before.

'I want to see my wife and daughter. I know they're here.'

'And who would you be referring to?'

'Don't play me for a fool. Emily and Abby. Get them down here.'

I have never seen Dad so angry. I hold tight onto Mum, to stop my shaking if anything.

'There is nobody by those names here,' says Sheena calmly.

Dad reacts by thumping the intercom. 'Damn you.' He walks off and shouts, 'I'll be back,' so loudly that the whole neighbourhood will have been able to hear.

Mum is as white as a ghost. I am still holding her arm firmly.

'We might have to move you.' Even Sheena appears spooked.

Our safe little bubble has come crashing down.

'Where to?' I ask.

'I'll figure something out. You go have lunch and try not to worry about it.'

Easier said than done. Worrying is all we do as we sit there pushing our food around the plate.

'I'm sure Sheena will find us somewhere safe.' Mum nods sadly.

Half an hour later and the drama continues. Another buzz to the door, this time less urgent, more polite. Sheena answers it.

'Hello, how can I help you?'

'My name is Detective Stevens,' replies the voice.

'It's the detective,' shrieks Mum standing up and almost knocking over the table in the process. 'She's come to rescue us.' Out of the window I see the woman who came to our house that time, dressed in a smart suit, looking around cautiously.

'I'll buzz you in,' says Sheena and then turns to us. 'You can speak to her in my office.'

Mum is frozen to the spot like she doesn't know what to do next and like she can't believe this is happening.

'Come on, Mum,' I say dragging her along by the arm.

The detective climbs up the stairs and smiles at us. Sheena leads us into her office.

'I was told you weren't working on the case anymore.'

'I've gone undercover. The less people knew the better. I couldn't risk your lives, or the operation.'

'So are you getting him for this?' I say hopefully.

'We're working on it. Believe me we are almost there but now is a good time to move you.'

'You heard about Dad turning up here? How did you know? How did he know we were here?'

'Whoa, whoa, Abby, too many questions. We're going to move you to a safe house.'

Mum doesn't say a word but her body language tells me everything I need to know.

'Are you okay Emily?'

She nods slowly.

'I think this has been too much for her,' I say, like I am the adult.

'You're doing well to look after her. I need you both to gather your things and come with me.'

'Now?'

'Yes Abby. It's not safe here anymore.'

I am disappointed to leave this happy home. I have no idea where we are going as we get in the car with the detective. I watch the people walking on the street with envy, so free. It's a long journey but for once I am appreciating the landscape. Maybe the beautiful mountains aren't so bad.

~

'Here we are folks,' says the detective like we are out on a day trip. I shake Mum to wake her. She raises her head sleepily and smiles.

'Where are we?'

'Scotland,' answers Detective Stevens.

'Scotland?' I shout loudly. 'I've never been there.'

'You have now. Enjoy.'

The house we've arrived outside is massive and there are no others in sight. The sky is dark and gloomy but I'm determined not to give into the despair inside me.

We step outside; it's good to stretch our legs after such a long journey. We follow her as she unlocks the door. I wonder if there are others in there.

'You'll be safe here. No one is going to find you.'

The large lounge is welcoming with its big, old fire place and the soft brown armchairs make it look like something out of a home interior magazine.

The stairs creak as we walk up the stairs.

'Here this is your room,' the detective gives me a knowing look, there is something she is not telling us.

Before I can question her the door slowly opens and a familiar face sits on the bed.

It doesn't take my brain long to catch up. 'Beth,' I cry out. Mum almost knocks me over to get in the door.

'Beth,' she cries. Beth gets up, smiling. 'But we were told you didn't make it?' She touches her face all over. Beth laughs.

'We thought you were dead,' I say grabbing hold of her in a hug. I don't want to ever let her go again. Tears are falling down from my eyes before I can stop them.

'We had to keep Beth safe,' insists the detective. 'Don't be angry at her.'

But we are far from mad. We cling to her in an emotional mess. The sister I thought was dead who is now alive - again.

## Abby - July 2018

I still can't believe Beth is alive. None of us slept that first night. Mum spent most of the night staring at her in case she disappeared again. We cried a lot. Mum had been falling apart recently but now it seems a light has gone on in her head. She is smiling. We can see hope again. We will get through this.

'I've got bad news and good news.' We are gathered together in the lounge sitting by the roaring fire listening intently to what the detective has to say.

'The good news is that we've got enough evidence to arrest Jack.'

'That's great,' says Beth happily. I never thought I'd be happy to see my Dad be arrested, but it couldn't be better news.

'But the bad news is he's gone on the run.'

'What?' we all exclaim at the same time.

'But you'll find him won't you?' I ask anxiously.

'We're working on it. We've got everyone we can on this. We're doing a press release right now. His face is going to be all over the news. He won't be able to get away.'

Later on we switch on the TV and Dad's face stares out at us. My Dad of fifteen years, the man I thought was kind and funny, brave and loving, now a wanted man. I reach out for Mum's and Beth's hands, mine shaking. They smile bravely.

'It'll be alright,' says Beth. I nod.

Later on we gaze at the TV, numbed by the news.

'Jack Kimmings, 42, is on the run from police. Do not approach this man if you see him,' the strangeness of seeing the familiar newsreader reporting about my Dad. 'Others in the ring have already been arrested.'

Flashing images of other men appear on the screen.

'Michael.' Beth stares at the screen, reaching out for it. I know she still misses him.

'Are you alright Beth?' I ask tentatively.

'Fine,' she answers quickly. 'I'm glad they've caught him.' But her tone suggests she is not fine about it. Mum switches off the TV.

'Let's do something else,' Mum suggests. Beth looks shell-shocked. Like me I guess she is still trying to process the idea of our father being responsible for such horrible acts.

That night I worry. I worry that he will never get caught and this nightmare will never be over. I lay awake staring at the ceiling tracing the shadows from the curtains until I can do it no more.

I get up and peer outside. The darkness is complete, not a street light or house light in sight. It scares me that I can see nothing. I want to see what is coming. I imagine him hiding out in the trees, ready to break into our house.

'Abby?' Mum startles me from behind.

'What are you doing up?'

'I could ask you the same thing.'

'I couldn't sleep.'

'Me neither.'

'How about a cuddle in bed?'

I get into bed and Mum climbs in next to me just like when I was a small child. Her body is warm and comforting; having someone else next to me is making me feel better already.

'It'll be alright.' She is trying hard to be convincing. I nuzzle into her like a lion cub while she strokes my hair gently.

I must have fallen asleep because the next thing I know sunlight is streaming through the curtains. Mum is still next to me, snoring quietly. For a moment I've forgotten the situation we are in and enjoy the moment with her but then it comes crashing back into my mind.

I get up, catching myself in the mirror as I go by. My hair hangs like it hasn't been brushed in days.

A knock at the door startles me and I freeze halfway down the stairs.

'Emily, it's me,' comes the detective's voice and I can breathe again. I rush down the rest of the wooden stairs, nearly slipping on the last few steps.

'Coming,' I call.

'You're not Emily.'

'No, she's still in bed.'

Detective Steven's face has the look of someone who has been awake all night, the sleepy eyes, the slight smile that seems an effort.

'You're here early.'

'Don't know whether it's early or late.' She smiles wearily.

'You have news?'

'I do.' Her expression brightens suddenly. I feel hope. 'Can you go and get your Mum?'

I want to shake it out of her; I desperately need to know but reluctantly I run upstairs to get Mum. She is sleeping so peacefully that I don't want to disturb her but I do anyway. I sit next to her and whisper gently:

'Mum, Mum, wake up. The detective's here.' She opens

her eyes slowly, confused and trying to make sense of it.

'- detective. Is it bad news?'

'No idea. She wouldn't tell me anything.'

Still in her pyjamas, she gets out of bed quickly and runs down the stairs. The detective is sitting there patiently when we arrive.

'What's the news?' Mum asks desperately.

'Jack's been caught.'

'Thank goodness.' Thoughts of what this will mean to us races through my mind. 'We can go home?'

'Not yet. He might get bail. We need to keep you safe for a little while longer, just until the trial.'

I nod. Desperate as I am to get home, I wonder if home will ever feel the same.

'I know this is hard folks. But we're almost there.'

I nod again through tears. Beth walks slowly down the stairs with a questioning expression.

'They got him.'

We fall into each other's arms in tears. Finally it's going to be good again.

That night I hear Mum on the phone to Uncle Pete. I don't think she's spoken to him for months.

'Emily,' he shouts out when he hears her voice. 'Where have you been?' His voice echoes around the room. 'Why didn't you tell ME where you were going?'

'Jack thought it would be safer. The less people knew the better.'

'I bloody knew he was a criminal. Didn't I always say?'

'Yes, Pete, you were right about him.'

Typical! Uncle Pete would be right.

**Beth - November 2018**

'Mr Kimmings, how do you plead?'

'Not guilty.'

Mum gasps next to me as I clench my fists. I can't

believe after everything he's denying it.

Seeing my father standing there in the dock makes this seem so real. I think we are still struggling to believe that Dad was behind it all. Mum clutches my arm and smiles.

Abby looks shocked by the whole thing. She turned sixteen yesterday, not a time to celebrate your big birthday. Another birthday that will have to be delayed. Mum promised we'd celebrate properly when this is over and the end is so close now.

Michael's trial finished last week. Traumatic does not even get close to how I felt about it. I know I was supposed to feel relieved, another criminal off the street, but this was Michael, my Michael. I could barely meet his eye as he sat in the dock, his face full of fear. I was shaking when he took the stand and he was asked 'Michael, tell us how you met Mr Kimmings?'

'I was short of money, down on my luck if you like. He was there when I needed him.' I felt sick when I heard him say those words. 'I met him at the pub. He told me he had a job for me. He told me it was all legal, above board. I believed him.'

'Why did you not walk away when you found out what it was?'

Michael sighed. 'It was good money. Then he gave me his daughter and I fell in love. I didn't mean to fall for her.' He was looking directly at me as he said this. 'It wasn't part of the plan. It would have been easier if she'd been like the others.' Tears began streaming down my face at this point. I thought I was going to lose control completely.

But I made it through it somehow. I don't know if I was relieved or sad when I heard the sentence he'd got, ten years. It was justifiable, sure, but he *loved* me. I knew he did. That meant something to me. It wasn't all lies. His last words before he was carried off were 'Beth I love you. Please give me another chance.'

'Bastard, how could he even say such a thing?'

screeched Mum.

I didn't answer. How could I tell her that for a moment I had considered it? That after the terrible things he'd done I had thought about visiting him in prison.

There was barely enough time to get over that before Dad's trial started. Now I sit facing him wondering if I will feel the same emotions that I did for Michael. Will I feel sad when he goes down for ten years? But it's more complicated than that, surely? His role was much bigger, but he is still my father.

At the mention of my name I tune back in to the proceedings.

'Mr Kimmings, why get your daughter Beth involved? Surely that was a risk?' He shrugs, I am just another girl to him. How could he have used me in such a way?

'She's good looking. Michael liked her, unfortunately too much. This is his fault,' he says angrily. 'He lost his nerve due to *love,* stupid boy. He doesn't even know what love is.'

Next to me I find Mum is breathing heavily, unable to comprehend the husband she once knew now being so cold hearted.

'So basically you're saying you're not sorry. You're just sorry you got caught.' He pauses and we all know that is the truth.

'I can't do this anymore,' whispers Mum, struggling to hold the tears in.

I squeeze her arm lightly. 'We can.'

It almost breaks our hearts to hear of the hideous things he has done. I want to leap up and shake him to make him understand how much he has hurt us but I fear it will do no good. There is no empathy left in him.

Day in and day out we endure his trial. It's almost too much but we survive because we have to see this out. We have to bring closure. The final day. We hold hands in solidarity.

This ends now.

'Mr Kimmings,' the judge begins, 'I cannot even begin to understand why a seemingly respectable and intelligent man felt the need to set up such a "business".' His words wash over me and my mind drifts. That my father is the mastermind of this is terrifying. I refocus in time to hear the judge say: 'Your crimes are horrendous and for that you must pay. I sentence you to twenty years in prison.'

Mum squeezes my hand hard. 'Twenty years!' she mouths to me. Detective Stevens told us it wasn't likely to be that long, so even her face is full of shock. She recovers and gives out a little cheer, for her this is a big win. I expect she'll be out celebrating tonight, drinking champagne to celebrate, but who would blame her. I don't hear any more of what the judge says. I am still processing what he said. In twenty years, he'll be sixty four, I'll be forty two, the same age he is now. Abby will be thirty five, all of us moved on with our lives. Twenty years is a long time but less time than he has been profiting from girls like me.

The inevitable tears flow down my cheeks, tears of sadness, anger, relief - I don't know anymore. Abby buries her head in my lap.

'We're free,' she whispers. I wonder if we'll ever be free from the lasting effects of this nightmare.

Across the courtroom I see a glimpse of a familiar face. A slight smile, a whole host of memories invading my mind. When she wanders over, the smartly dressed woman stops. I hug her before she can stop me.

'Lily, you look different.' She is no longer the gaunt girl who I once knew but her bright smile is the same.

'So do you. You look fantastic.' She's just being kind but I appreciate the sentiment.

'What are you up to now?'

'I'm proper boring now, steady job, decent boyfriend.'

'Boring's good though, right?'

'Absolutely.' She hasn't lost the spark. 'I need to go, but it was great seeing you.'

She strides confidently out of the door turning only to give me one last grin.

~

Afterwards, we celebrate with Uncle Pete and Judy. Pete is more than happy that my Dad is going down for a long time. He never liked him. I could never understand why. He greets me with a long hug. I pull away and push him back.

'Seriously Uncle Pete, can you stop touching me all the time. I don't like it.' I can see Abby grinning at me from behind his back, congratulating me on saying exactly what we've all been thinking for a long time. He is taken aback and stumbles a little.

'But- '

'It's not the 1970s anymore. Hugging people indiscriminately is not acceptable.'

It is the first time I have seen him speechless.

**Abby - January 2019**

'Home sweet home.' I never thought I'd hear those words again. Mum is standing in the lounge of our new house, proud, happy.

'What do you think?'

'It's small,' I answer with a grin.

'Oh get over it you,' says Beth, chucking her teddy at me.

'Seriously, it's lovely Mum.'

'I know it's not as big as our other house but it's ours and we are safe.'

Safe, the most important thing for us. The word has never been so poignant as now. I want to forgive Dad. My RE teacher always used to say forgiveness is important, not for them but for you, so that you can move on. But I'm struggling. How do you forgive someone who is not remorseful, only sorry he got caught? Right there on the dock I searched his face for a sense of sorrow when he met my eye but there was nothing but a stone cold stare. It nearly broke my heart. My *loving* father. Was it all lies? Did he ever really care for me? Did he ever love Mum?

I begged Mum not to send me back to school. I mean I've been through enough life lessons, surely I have had all the education I need but at least it is to a new school. A fresh start, a chance for us to move on.

Sometimes I imagine the other kids are looking at me thinking that I'm some kind of freak. They must know the truth, it was in the papers. It's big news. It's not every day they break up a grooming ring. Big success for the police; big trauma for us. But if they know, they don't say anything, and for that I am grateful.

'Knock, knock.' The door, which is slightly ajar, moves as Uncle Pete and Judy enter the house. 'Hi sis.' He hugs Mum. He goes to hug Beth but she moves away from him. 'Sorry I forgot you don't like that anymore.' I want to punch him for being so insensitive. 'Lovely place. When's the house warming party?'

'Give us a chance. We just got in,' laughs Mum. Beth and I exchange looks. We are older now, Uncle Pete's friendly banter may be that for him but we both know he needs to get with the times. He acts like everyone is as touchy feely as him.

'How's the new job going?' Judy asks.

'I'm loving it,' replies Mum enthusiastically. 'It's different. I don't know why I thought working in an office was a good thing.'

Mum works in a book shop now. She spends her days talking to other nerds about how great books are. Beth is a waitress, for now anyway. She's still considering her options. She also spends a lot of time in her room with the curtains shut.

Last week that detective came round. We were surprised to see her again, I thought the trial was the last time we'd ever see her. She told us extra details, including that Dad had an apartment in London, a very expensive one apparently. Mum was disgusted, all those times he'd stayed away on "business" when he was just there with goodness knows who. I dread to think of it now, who he was with: girls, women, couples - doesn't bear thinking about.

'I bought us a takeaway,' says Uncle Pete, producing bags of fish and chips. I sigh, how many times have I told him I don't like fish and chips? 'We need to fatten you up,' he glances over at Beth. 'You're far too thin these days.'

Beth rolls her eyes and clenches her fists but smiles anyway. I squeeze her hand to offer my support.

As we sit in our new home, full of half-opened boxes and furniture in the wrong places, I think about the journey we have been through. I couldn't have imagined any of this, but it happened. It was horrible but we are stronger because of it. While Dad sits and rots in prison, hopefully getting beaten up by some other nonce, we continue to enjoy the good food and freedom. Freedom, something Dad denied us for so long.

But now we are truly free.

**Beth - January 2019**

*'How do you find the defendant Michael Stevens?'*

*'Guilty.' I watch his face, he is a deflated man.*

*'I love you,' he mouths at me.*

The front of the building has changed, done up since I was last here. It takes me a while to figure how to get in as everything's in a different place. The receptionist greets me with a smile.

'Lovely to meet you. Mrs Dodd told us you were coming. We've heard so much about you.'

Heard what? That I squandered my education for an older man.

'Love the hair.'

My newly dyed pink hair is vibrant once more.

'If you sit in the waiting area, I'll let Mrs Dodd know you are here.'

I seat myself in the soft red chair next to the glossy prospectus ready to sell me my old school. *High expectations, outstanding Ofsted rating, 98% A/A* grades.* Who was the poor bugger who didn't get an "A"? I bet they don't announce how many dropped out due to grooming? The building may have changed but the pressure is still the same. I'm glad to be out of it. I can already feel the panic of not being good enough rising within me.

To be honest I was surprised when Mrs Dodd rang me a few weeks ago to ask me to come in. I resisted at first. Why would I want to relive everything I went through but she insisted.

'You're an inspiration,' she said. 'You survived a horrible experience.'

I'm not sure that makes me an inspiration. I was lucky. But despite that anything that helps other people not to screw up is a good thing.

I'm so nervous. I can't believe I'm actually this nervous. I haven't eaten all morning but then I don't eat much these days anyway.

'You'll be fine,' says Mrs Dodd who has appeared next to me.

She doesn't seem to have changed in the last ten years. In fact she hasn't aged at all, and she still has that kind smile.

'I'm so grateful for you coming today. It's such an important thing you are doing.'

She leads me to the assembly hall, which is the same. Memories of sitting cross-legged on the floor desperate to stretch out my legs flash before me. We were so keen to get to Year Eleven so we could sit on chairs. The funny thing was though, once we got there we realised the chairs weren't all that. They were pretty uncomfortable too.

'So you will stand here and in a minute the girls will be brought in. Be yourself, be honest. They need to hear it.'

I have practised what I am going to say so many times. Too gory? Not gory enough?

'Shock tactics is the way to go,' said Abby when we discussed it. 'How many times have you played on the railway line?'

'Never.'

'Exactly because you probably had that talk at primary school where the girl got her legs chopped off.'

'Yes. I remember that,' I laughed.

'Exactly, you remember it because it shocked you.'

She's right. So I kept in the gory details. No point in glamorising something when I'm trying to stop *them* doing it.

A teacher pops her head round the door.

'Is it okay to bring them in?' She's young, I don't recognise her.

'Yes, of course.'

I watch as the Year Ten and Eleven girls file in, shirts tucked in, skirts pulled down to the right length. Some smile at me, others stare at me curiously. They sit on the chairs put out for them and wait eagerly, faces turned towards me, alert. When the last one has sat down, I take a deep breath.

'My name is Beth Kimmings. I've come to tell you my story, so you don't make the same mistakes.'

The End

# ABOUT THE AUTHOR

Vicky was born in South Essex and after quite a few years moving around, she settled in North Essex where she now lives with her husband, David, and teenage daughters, Hannah and Megan.

Vicky did a degree in History, American Studies, and English, and has been been a teacher for fourteen years. She is currently teaching English at a secondary school in Suffolk.

She has always loved writing and has been on numerous writing courses. Powerless is her first novel and a dream come true.

NO ONE SAW IT COMING
#STOP THE GLITCH
CHRIS MALONE

ON TIME
PAM JARVIS

www.ingramcontent.com/pod-product-compliance
Ingram Content Group UK Ltd.
Pitfield, Milton Keynes, MK11 3LW, UK
UKHW041955190726
13854UKWH00005B/1975